The Murder of Norman Ware

First published by Jacana Media (Pty) Ltd in 2012

10 Orange Street
Sunnyside
Auckland Park 2092
South Africa
(+27 11) 628 3200
www.jacana.co.za

ISBN 978-1-4314-0444-5

Cover design by publicide
Set in Warnock 12/15.5pt
Printed by Ultra Litho (Pty) Ltd, Johannesburg
Job no. 001866

See a complete list of Jacana titles at www.jacana.co.za

The Murder of Norman Ware

by Rosamund Kendal

Chapter One

THE MURDER OF ADVOCATE Norman Ware caused great consternation among the residents of the exclusive San La Mer eco-estate. This was not because Advocate Norman Ware was a particularly well-liked man, nor was it because he held any sort of standing in the San La Mer community, despite the fact that he was a renowned and highly regarded advocate. The murder of Advocate Norman Ware (and he was never called anything other than Advocate Norman Ware: never simply Norman, or Mr Ware, or even, in the private-school manner, Ware) caused a furore in the luxurious gated community because it was not supposed to happen. The residents of San La Mer paid steeply but never reluctantly to ensure that such things did not happen. Their collective, exorbitant levies subsidised the electric fence around the perimeter of the estate and the infrared beams that sensed any human movement where it should not be. They paid for the security guards who patrolled the estate twenty-four/seven and manned both of the entrance gates, carefully screening access to the estate. The pay-off for the residents of San La Mer, the pay-off for the expense and for the hassle of phoning the control room for a unique access code every time one of their friends wanted to pop in for coffee or sundowners, was that they were assured that they would not be murdered in their homes. Advocate Norman Ware's death both made that reassurance extremely tenuous and devalued their properties overnight. Of course, it was also the manner in which Advocate Norman Ware was murdered that caused alarm.

But the residents of San La Mer were needlessly worried. They could have gone back to their marble and cherry-wood mansions, their sedate games of golf, their gin-and-tonics and tipsy trivia-quiz evenings, without another thought of Advocate Norman Ware. Their contained, carefully constructed lives of illusion need not have been disturbed. And perhaps, after the dissipation of the hype surrounding the murder, they would not be. Perhaps the disquiet surrounding Advocate Norman Ware's untimely and ignominious death would be transient, like a ripple on a lake, disturbing the still, glassy surface for a few seconds and then disappearing completely, leaving behind no trace of its source. Because the fact was that Advocate Norman Ware's murder was the culmination of a series of seemingly unrelated, purely random events. The chance of something like it ever happening again was infinitesimal. Besides, the motive for Advocate Norman Ware's murder – if indeed something so at the whim of coincidence could be labelled a murder – was not armed robbery or hijacking. His death was not the result of a paid hit; he was no corrupt mining magnate or overly inquisitive journalist. The motive for his murder was the oldest and purest motive, one repeated throughout history; it was an inexplicable, unreasonable motive; a lonely, private and desperate motive. The motive behind Advocate Norman Ware's murder was, quite simply, love.

But none of the residents knew that when his body was found by one of the groundsmen near the communal swimming pool early in the morning of the third of November, and so there followed among the residents of the estate an inordinate amount of distress, frowning, hand wringing, and phoning of financial advisers and lawyers.

—•—

Jackson Ngombo left work early on the afternoon of the second of November, as he did every Wednesday. His contract allowed him to take off a half day on Wednesdays in order to compensate for his having to work every Sunday morning from five thirty to eleven, mowing the greens so that golfers scheduled to spend their day of rest playing on the world-class San La Mer golf course would have perfect surfaces from which to putt their insignificant little white balls. It didn't enter his mind to question the legitimacy of this arrangement, even though he had to wake up at three o'clock on a Sunday morning in order to get to work by five thirty. In fact, having Wednesday afternoons off suited him because it gave him the opportunity to meet up with his girlfriend, Pretty.

Pretty was as attractive as her name implied. Few onlookers, struck by the immediate force of her beauty, would notice the hardness that played on her lips for a split second before they broke into a smile. Even fewer would realise that the depths of her cocoa eyes could not be plumbed; that they were shallow and glassy, the windows to her soul shut tightly. There was a darkness to Pretty's beauty, a side to it that was unnervingly reminiscent of the story of the Flying Dutchman or the legend of Van Hunks, that was somehow suggestive of a bargain with the devil.

When Noluthando Gwala had been pregnant with Pretty, she began to swell up in a way that she had not with any of her five other children. Her fingers and toes had been transformed into sausages. Her belly had become a tense drum streaked with purple-blue veins. Her breasts had turned pendulous and her face had become puffy and round, like the full moon. She had eventually lumbered to the local clinic, fearful that her skin would split if she grew any bigger. The doctor at the clinic, an overworked intern with bloodshot brown eyes and the tremor of a habitual coffee drinker, had mumbled something about her blood pressure and sent her by ambulance to King Edward Hospital, where white-coated specialists cut her baby from her womb. As the infant had left her body, Noluthando began to shrink. The loose skin that had been left by the newborn's departure hung in shrivelled folds over her belly and around her ankles and wrists, so that it looked as though she were a body inhabiting another's skin.

As Noluthando looked down on her perfect daughter – born with a head full of thick, black curls; eyes brown and wide and long-lashed like a cow; a rosebud mouth; and flushed pink cheeks – she sighed in awe, not realising for one moment that this tiny being, on her dramatic exit from the womb, had stolen all of her mother's loveliness.

Noluthando, who was not used to the perfection of a Caesar baby, but knew only the boggy, coned heads and squashed faces of infants who had been forced down a narrow, hostile birth canal, knew without any doubt that the little doll in her arms would break many hearts in her lifetime. She did not know then that her heart would be one of those broken, and that her husband, unable to bear the ugliness of his once-beautiful wife, would take a new wife and discard Noluthando, like an item of clothing for which he no longer had any use. But that would happen in the years to come. At the moment of her daughter's birth, Noluthando believed she had been blessed, and she had named her daughter Pretty.

Whether it was because she had stolen her mother's beauty or because her mother had been foolish enough to name her as she did, Pretty was destined for unhappiness. Too beautiful for any man to risk taking as his wife, she would become mistress to a string of men. She would learn at a young age the value of her sexuality, but only later would she learn the price. Years of manipulating men would leave her unable to trust anyone, and with no knight in shining armour to resurrect the scraps of leftover idealism from her childhood, she would become increasingly disillusioned and bitter, until eventually she would tolerate only those relationships that were based entirely on material value.

But now, when we see her waiting at the shebeen for Jackson early on that Wednesday afternoon, she is sixteen years old and in the prime of her beauty. Betrayal and cynicism have not yet taken their full toll on her appearance. She has glossy copper-blonde extensions on her hair, falling midway down her back. Her eyes are lined in thick black eyeliner, and the sensuous fullness of her lips is highlighted in glittering pink. She has been to the beauty salon, for men pay well to have attractive, well-groomed mistresses, and she is sporting long, bright-red acrylic nails. What turns men's heads, though, is not so much her external appearance as the confidence and sexual energy that she exudes. She is unashamedly for sale to the highest bidder.

Jackson met Pretty at the door to the shebeen, as he had done every Wednesday for the past three months. He kissed her briefly, resting his hands, while their lips touched, on the firm roundness of her buttocks, and then went inside to buy some quarts of Black Label beer. It was dark inside the shebeen, and muggy. The air was thick with cigarette smoke and sweat and alcohol. Men sat on upturned crates. Some talked loudly, gesticulating and laughing; others were silent. Near the entrance, one man had passed out and lay on the dirt floor. His body was spreadeagled, his limbs messily flung out, and Jackson shivered, reminded suddenly of the victim of a hit-and-run accident that he had once glimpsed while passing in a taxi. Usually Jackson would linger for a while with Pretty at his side, having a drink and showing her off, but on that Wednesday the air in the shebeen seemed to want to choke him. He coughed, trying to get rid of the thickness in his throat, but it refused to budge. For the first time, he noticed the despair that hung around the drinking hole, beneath the smoke and the harsh laughter. It was like a ghost, hovering on the periphery, and Jackson felt that, if he stayed, that despair might inhabit him and take possession of his soul. Perhaps that was what had happened to these men, sitting drinking in the middle of the day, and their whores, spilling over them in drunken disregard. He paid for his beers quickly and hurried out of the shebeen.

As Jackson stepped into the sunlight, he noticed that his skin was covered in tiny beads of sweat. Pretty began to nag, asking him why he was in such a hurry to go and moaning that she wanted to stay at the shebeen, and for the first time since they had started seeing each other, he growled at her, warning her to shut up and listen to him.

Later, in the taxi on the way to his house, he felt guilty for having shouted at her and he snuggled close to her body, trying to apologise, but Pretty was sulking and refused his advances. He had never seen her petulant and it irritated him, because it was due to him that she had such fancy hair, nails and make-up. Without all that he had given her, she would be like any other teenage schoolgirl. The thought did cross his mind later on in the afternoon, once his wife, Gugu, had walked in on him and Pretty having sex, that if he had listened to Pretty and stayed at the shebeen, his wife would never have found out about his affair.

Gugu was not supposed to come home early on a Wednesday afternoon. She usually arrived home at six o'clock, by which time Jackson had finished with Pretty. On Wednesday the second of November, however, Gugu's employer, who had cancer, had collapsed and had had to be rushed to hospital in an ambulance, and so the shaken Gugu had been given the afternoon off, which was how she happened to stumble upon her husband and a beautiful teenager making love in her bed. Gugu's immediate reaction, when she saw her naked husband, was to laugh. He looked ridiculously comical, with his bare, pimply bottom bouncing up and down in the air: a middle-aged man trying to prove his manhood to a little dressed-up doll. Her laughter appeared to scare the copulating couple more than any shouting and screaming would have. The girl scrambled off the bed and grabbed her discarded clothes from the floor, lifting them to cover her naked labia. Jackson sat still, unable to decide how to respond. It was as though Gugu's stare had turned him to stone, an ignoble and tragicomic David posed upon the rumpled bedclothes.

Gugu's laughter turned to anger, a fury that boiled in her stomach and made her want to vomit, that caused her hands to shake and her heart to take flight, but she refused to succumb to it. Instead, she made herself walk calmly to the pine cupboard on the other side of the room. It was second-hand, a gift from her employer, and the scruffy remains of stickers, the full cast of Ben 10, were still visible on the doors. They had never bothered her before, because she had seen the cupboard solely in terms of its function, but now the demons seemed to be mocking her and leering at her. How long had they been witness to this debauchery? she wondered. Gugu packed some clothes for herself and the children into an old tog bag, enough to last them for several days. As she walked out, she told Jackson that she would send her brother to fetch the rest of her things on Saturday. He was not to expect her back soon.

When Gugu told her employer, Angela, about the incident a few days later, she realised that she had suspected the affair for a while. 'Black men are like that,' she told her employer bitterly. 'They can't keep only one woman. They have to have lots of women, but I don't want that. I don't want a man who wastes his money buying another woman instead of paying for food and clothes for his children. You wouldn't understand because white men aren't like that.' Angela had not known how to respond. She had wanted to tell Gugu that many white men are like that; that possibly they had just been forced to be more discreet.

———•———

It took Jackson a long time to get up from the bed once Gugu had walked out with the battered Health & Racquet

Club tog bag slung over her shoulder. Pretty had dressed and sat waiting for him on the step at the door of the one-roomed house, sipping a beer. The afternoon sun came in through the doorway and framed her, so that she looked like a movie character with burnished copper hair, but Jackson was now unmoved by her beauty. He wanted her gone, wanted her evil temptation as far from him as possible.

Perhaps Pretty was intuitive enough to sense Jackson's mood because she picked up her handbag, the diamanté-studded silver one that she had bought from Mr Price that morning with money Jackson had given her, and walked out into the road. She was hoping that Jackson would call her back, but he didn't. He didn't even get up to watch her walk down the street, two hours earlier than she usually did on a Wednesday afternoon.

All of this – the debacle with Pretty and Gugu; the knowledge that his wife had walked out on him; the fact that he would not see his five-year-old son and two-year-old daughter again for an indeterminate length of time – resulted in Jackson drinking far too much that Wednesday night, which in turn meant that he was late for work on Thursday morning, the third of November.

Jackson was employed by a large landscaping company that maintained both the gardens and the golf course within the San La Mer estate. Usually, Jackson worked on the golf course and had to be at the estate early in order to mow the fairways and greens before the golfing day began. It would not be unreasonable to say that Jackson enjoyed his work. He liked driving the powerful, automated lawnmowers. He enjoyed donning earmuffs, protective glasses and a thick plastic apron and attacking the unruly edges of the course with a weed-eater. He took pleasure in the washing of the machines after a day's work: hosing down the lawnmower after carefully removing the plastic grass-collection containers from the base; unwinding the cords from the weed-eater and wiping down the body; hanging the edge-trimmer on a thick steel hook in the wall of the maintenance shed beside all the other weed-eaters and branch-cutters and edge-trimmers; and then sharing a cigarette with a colleague. There was something about the power of the machines that excited him and raised him above the level of ordinary gardener. But on the morning of the third of November, he arrived at work late, and so he was delegated to the landscaping section as opposed to the golf-course side and issued with a pair of grass clippers from the maintenance shed (all the weed-eaters had long before been handed out). Along with the grass clippers, he was given his first written warning, which engendered renewed thoughts of anger towards both Pretty and Gugu. It might have been that anger, although it could equally have been the beer he had consumed the previous evening, that made his head feel as though it was going to burst and caused his eyes to burn in the sunlight. But he was not at all nauseous until he stumbled on the body.

Jackson's job for the day was to trim manually the edges of the flowerbeds in the communal pool area. The communal pool area incorporated three pools (a large one in which exercise fanatics could swim lengths and kids could play water polo; a smaller, kidney-shaped one with submerged seating in which lovers could pet and women display themselves; and a round, shallow one in which toddlers could waddle); a small restaurant that sold light meals, sodas, cocktails and wine by the glass; ablution facilities with toilets and showers; and a sunning area complete with deck chairs and umbrellas. The pool area was one of the attributes of San La Mer that made it such an exclusive and sought-after estate. It was to this pool area that Jackson was banished after arriving late at work. It is important to note here that what was considered late in terms of Jackson's arrival at work was relatively early in many other respects. In fact, the murder scene was discovered at eight forty-five, which was far too early for any of the San La Mer residents to have even thought about making the leisurely trip down to the pools.

Jackson had been clipping sky-blue plumbago bushes for half an hour before the heat, superimposed upon his hangover, became intolerable. Had he waited for fifteen more minutes, had he tolerated the heat for a quarter of an hour longer before deciding to find a drink, the restaurant staff would have arrived and he could have begged a glass of water from them instead of going to the men's bathroom in search of a drink and inadvertently stumbling across a murder scene. But fate would have Jackson punished more severely for his infidelity than with a simple hangover, and so it was that he opened the swing door to the men's ablution facility and discovered the body of Advocate Norman Ware.

The sight of Advocate Norman Ware's body immediately made Jackson fiercely nauseous, so much so that he had to run out of the bathroom to avoid vomiting on a crime scene. He retched instead onto the very hedges he was supposed to be neatening that morning. Once he had finished hurling the remainders of the previous night's beer onto the blue plumbago and yellow-and-orange Cape honeysuckle, he sprinted to the parking area of the pools, where he knew a security guard was sitting on a bench listening to music on his cellphone. He did not return to the bathroom to check whether he had been hallucinating, or if someone was playing a sick joke, or if a Halloween costume had been unthinkingly stashed away on the floor of the ablution facility. He did not want to risk having to see again what he had seen once. Even so, although he had been with the body of Advocate Norman Ware for no longer than thirty seconds, he would forever more be haunted by images of the corpse's disfigured genitals whenever he thought of sex. Advocate Norman Ware would ultimately be the cause of Jackson's erectile dysfunction, and although Jackson would visit doctors and sangomas, and even faith healers from Somalia, it would never be cured. It was as though Gugu had cursed him with a distinctly warped and very cruel punishment for his philandering.

Chapter Two

LET US TAKE A BRIEF HIATUS, a short break from the narrative, to examine in a little more detail the setting in which the murder of Advocate Norman Ware took place. It is fair to say that no murder is completely separate from its background. Even if a corpse has been moved to another place, the choice of that setting gives the investigator some insight into the murder and the murderer. A body that has been chopped up and stored in a chest freezer, which in turn has been stashed away in a storage unit, implies a planned murder. It also suggests that the murderer has certain means at his or her disposal. Alternatively, a murder that has taken place at a taxi rank at night and in which the bullet-riddled body has merely been discarded there, to be found at dawn, implies a completely different sort of crime and motive. The same can be said for a body found on a semen-stained bed in a hotel room or for remains found in a burnt car beside a warehouse at the docks. Not only does the setting of a murder provide the physical evidence – the fingerprints, DNA, and so on – but it gives an indication of the more subtle details often necessary to discover the motive behind the murder. It is representative of the social milieu in which the murder took place, with all of its associated nuances and undertones, and no less so in the case of the murder of Advocate Norman Ware.

The following is an extract from the San La Mer sales brochure:

San La Mer is South Africa's prime residential destination. Situated on the stunning East Coast, a mere forty-five minutes north of Durban, it is every discerning property buyer's dream! The eco-estate offers a world-class golf course and country club, two tennis courts, a luxurious pool area and two fully licensed restaurants, all with diplomatic-level security. This is State of the Art Living at its best! Come and emigrate to San La Mer now!

This text is printed on glossy paper and accompanied by beautiful photographs taken at sunset. At a cursory glance, the appeal is obvious, and since many people prefer to skim over the surface of life, sales in the estate are always good. A murder investigation, however, has the annoying tendency to scratch and pick at that smooth surface, creating unwelcome ruffles and cracks from which inevitably escape certain truths that people would rather avoid, which was probably another reason for the consternation surrounding Advocate Norman Ware's murder, even if it was only on a subconscious level. Because the truth was that the foundations of the San La Mer estate were cemented in corruption and that lies, decay and extortion lay very shallow beneath the perfectly manicured grounds.

The name 'San La Mer' is often incorrectly believed to be of French origin, and the ignorant flippantly translate it in their minds as 'beside the sea' or 'on the beachfront'. For some, the name conjures up images of the French

Riviera; for others, of cabanas beside a tropical island paradise. If one takes the time to translate the name properly, however, one soon realises that there is no French word *san*. There is the word *sans*, which means 'without', so the nearest translation is 'without the sea', which conjures up slightly less appealing images. Where does the name come from, then? Were the developers sloppy in their nomenclature? Not in the least. The developers merely took their clients for fools. 'San La Mer' is an anagram of the name of the large investment company that developed the estate, originally during the apartheid years, as a holiday destination for its privileged directors, many of whom were also prominent politicians at the time. After the fall of the apartheid government, the further development of the estate was taken over, in a series of business deals that made four new millionaires, by a more politically correct property development consortium. Of course, the group consisted of the same members as before, but a black chairman now headed it. And the name of the consortium was strategically changed to Amatola Trading and Development.

As early as 1987, when the first white wooden pegs were being hammered into the ground to demarcate separate erven on the estate, a complaint was filed at the local municipality. The complainant was a certain Joseph Bhengu, and the complaint was that the land being developed was an ancient Zulu burial site in which the remains of the ancestors of his community were interred. Joseph's protests were ignored, and shortly thereafter he was imprisoned for two years for a petty crime that he may or may not have committed. He was released after the change in government, at which point he filed the complaint again, sure that development on the proposed estate would now be halted and that his ancestors would be allowed the peace and respect they deserved. Instead, his community was offered a large sum of money as payment for their acquiescence. Joseph disputed the decision taken by the community to accept the money. He knew that no good would come of desecrating a burial site, but he was powerless in the face of hunger and poverty.

Joseph was not the only person who tried to halt the development of the land on which the San La Mer estate was being built. A small group which called themselves 'Friends of the Coastal Forests' took Amatola Trading and Development to court in an attempt to save one of the last pockets of indigenous coastal forest on the east coast of South Africa. The gifts of a number of luxurious cars to certain members of the judiciary ensured that the court case was thrown out, and in a token gesture to pacify the press, the developers promised to make the proposed estate an eco-estate. No one questioned the logic of the development of a golf course on an eco-estate.

The murder of Advocate Norman Ware thus occurred against a neatly disguised background of corruption, bribery and ghosts. It was no wonder, then, that it would prove tricky to solve.

Although Tariq Pillay was not directly involved in the murder of Advocate Norman Ware, the crime might never have happened if he had not passed out on the bench in the parking area adjacent to the pools. Had he been doing his duty as security guard, which was to patrol the pool area and parking lot overnight, he might have heard Advocate Norman Ware's screams and possibly come to his rescue, or at least interrupted the murderer. As it was, at the time of the murder he was in a benzodiazepine-induced oblivion and the screams of the victim reached his ears as the distant cry of seagulls. He did not have the capacity in that state to question the likelihood of seagulls calling at three o'clock in the morning.

Contrary to what the police investigating the case believed, Tariq was not a habitual drug user. They briefly considered that he might have been drugged by the murderer, because of the high benzodiazepine levels found in his mandatory blood sample, but there was no evidence that he had been given the medication via the intravenous or intramuscular routes, and he was unable to provide a watertight story explaining how he was forced to swallow large numbers of oral benzodiazepines. In the end, the police had to presume that he was a prescription-drug addict and that he had allowed his addiction to interfere with his job as a security guard. One positive aspect to the situation, and possibly the only one, was that Tariq's high serum drug concentrations ruled him out as a suspect in the murder: there was no possibility, even if his weight was double what it was and his liver enzymes had the capacity of a chronic alcoholic, that he had been anything but comatose at the time of the murder.

Given that after the exposure of his role – or the lack thereof – in the murder of Advocate Norman Ware he was in any case going to be fired from the security company for which he worked, Tariq might as well have told the police the truth about how he came to have ingested the potent benzodiazepines, but perhaps he was too embarrassed. There is also the possibility that he thought it would look better on his curriculum vitae to have been fired for a prescription-drug addiction than for breaking-

and-entering and petty theft, although strictly speaking he did not break into the house. The door was unlocked and there were, arguably, extenuating circumstances. The pertinent point is that had Tariq been performing his duty effectively, the murder might never have been allowed to happen.

Ever since Tariq Pillay had started working for First Response Security, some four months before the murder, he had suffered from headaches. Initially he had put the ailment down to working night shifts, something that his body was not accustomed to, but when the headaches persisted after the completion of his first month of work, he had gone to his family doctor to make sure that the headaches were not caused by something serious. The doctor checked his blood pressure, which had been normal, and did some blood tests, which also came back as unremarkable, and after shining a light into Tariq's eyes, prodding his shoulders a couple of times and pushing on his temples, the doctor reassured Tariq that the headaches were caused by stress. Tariq agreed. This was, after all, his very first job since leaving school. The doctor gave Tariq some painkillers, and as long as Tariq took these, his headaches were controllable. One month later the headaches were still present and Tariq phoned the doctor's surgery for advice on whether he needed further tests. The doctor had shrugged off Tariq's questions and had written out a repeat script for Tariq for the analgesics. His doctor's lack of concern reassured Tariq that the headaches were of benign origin and Tariq had continued with the medication.

On the afternoon of the second of November, however, Tariq had not taken his tablets. The reason he had neglected to take his tablets was one of simple logistics.

Earlier in the day, while she had been ironing his uniform for him, Tariq's mother had dropped the iron on her toe. She had hobbled to her medicine cupboard in search of some paracetamol, but the bottle had been empty. With the throbbing pain of a subungual haematoma driving her to tears, she had sneaked into Tariq's room – he was still sleeping after having worked the night before – and had removed the bottle of painkillers from his bedside table. Tariq's mother had not returned the bottle to his room because she did not want to risk waking Tariq, but instead had left it on the shelf next to the front door, where she presumed that Tariq would see it on his way out to work.

Without the usual prompt of the plastic bottle of light green tablets on his bedside table, Tariq completely forgot about the pills, and only remembered them once he arrived at work and felt the beginnings of a headache stirring at the base of his neck. Panicking, he had searched through his rucksack, hoping that he had left the bottle in his bag or that an errant pill had escaped unnoticed. His bag contained only a grey fleece jersey, an umbrella, some cherry-flavoured chewing gum and a sandwich wrapped in cling film. By the time that he reached the San La Mer pool area, where he was supposed to be on duty for the night, Tariq was in agony and had lost his vision in one eye.

Tariq should have contacted his superior and explained the situation to him. Later, after he had been fired for being drugged on duty, his mother would ask him over and over again why he hadn't. The reason Tariq had failed to bring the matter to his superior was that he was concerned that he should not appear to be taking chances. He was still new enough in the job to be worried about the impression he was making. So, instead of contacting his boss and asking him for the night off, or even for a couple of loose Disprin or Panado, Tariq sat down on the bench and pressed his forehead with his palms, as though by applying pressure externally he could somehow ease the force from within. It did little to alleviate the pain, which was now becoming so severe that Tariq thought he might vomit. The only solution that came to Tariq seemed to lie in the house adjacent to the parking area.

There was only one house near the pools, and for the four months that Tariq had been working for First Response Security, he had never seen anyone go into or come out of this house. A light was visible from behind the curtains of one of the upstairs windows, but it was never turned off and shone continuously night and day. Tariq presumed that the house was a holiday home and that the light had been left on accidentally when its owners had packed up and left for their regular home. He also presumed that even though the house was probably used only for three weeks of the year, there must be a medicine cupboard or first-aid box somewhere inside. It would be easy enough, he thought, to slip in through a window and find some painkillers. Logically, since the security on the San La Mer estate was of almost diplomatic level, none of the houses were fitted with burglar alarms or even burglar bars. Had Tariq's brain not been so muddled by pain, he might have seen the pitfalls of his plan, but at that moment the house, with its possibility of analgesia, seemed to Tariq his only chance of salvation.

Tariq knocked on the door in case he had misread the situation and the house was, in fact, inhabited. There was no response after a minute, so Tariq turned the doorknob. He had not expected the door to open. He had imagined that he would have to pry open one of the large wooden sash windows and slip in through the gap. He had turned the doorknob merely as a token gesture, a habit almost, but the lock had clicked and the door had swung open.

The house was dark inside, and dusty, as befitted a house used only once a year for a wealthy family's summer vacation. The air was musty, stuffy, and smelt of rot and decay. Tariq took shallow breaths, irrationally fearing that if he breathed too deeply he would begin to decompose. The front door led into an open-plan kitchen and dining area. Tariq walked through the room, looking for a medicine cabinet. His feet echoed oddly in the quiet house and each step he took unsettled soft puffs of dust. There was nothing that resembled a first-aid kit or medicine chest in the main living area or in the guest toilet. He walked down a short passage and pushed open the door at the end. It was a guest room. Tariq looked hopefully inside the cupboards, but they were empty. He wanted to leave the house. There was something about it that disturbed him – something more than just the fact that he was trespassing and that it was creepy and full of cobwebs – but his headache was too bad for him to forgo his search. He knew that if he didn't find some medication to deaden the pain he would have a stroke, or something worse.

His grandmother had had a stroke when Tariq was ten. Half of her body had become seized up and her face had frozen into a distorted mask, but the abiding image that Tariq could not erase from his mind was that of the spit that continually dribbled from one corner of her mouth down her chin and onto the bib that Tariq's mother tied around her neck each morning. Tariq shuddered at the memory, at the thought that something similar might happen to him, and made his way to the staircase. It was as he reached the second storey that he realised what it was that was bothering him about the house: everything was sealed. There was tape over all the drains and taps; the air-conditioning ducts had been covered with sheets of newsprint; and there was duct tape around all of the windows. It was weird, freaky, and if Tariq had not seen the container of tablets on the dresser on the landing, he would have turned around and left immediately. As it was, he grabbed the tablets as quickly as he could and rushed down the stairs and back out of the house. In his pain and panic, he failed to notice that the container in his hand was similar, but not identical, to the box in which the analgesic Panamol usually came. He also failed to notice, as he shoved four of the tablets into his mouth, that they were of a different colour and size from the Panamol that he had taken on occasion in the past.

Tariq's brief foray did not go entirely unnoticed; there was a witness to his flirtation with petty crime. Tariq had been incorrect in his presumption that the house was a holiday home. There was, in fact, a permanent resident in the place. Cordelia Cupido had been living in the house for the past twenty months, although she did not own the property.

Two years before, Cordelia – or Delia, as her husband had always called her – had been happy. Her life had been as close to perfect as she could imagine it being. Looking back, Delia couldn't help wondering how two years could feel simultaneously like eternity and the blink of an eyelid. It seemed as though she had been stuck in this horrible prison of a house forever, but at the same time it felt as though, if she just closed her eyes, she could see every detail of the flowers – the bright yellow of the petals, the soft orange bumps of their centres, the tiny hairs on the grey-green stems – that she had been arranging moments before her life had collapsed, as though it had happened only yesterday. How was it possible for time to be so fluid, so easily manipulated by an unhappy mind? she wondered.

Two years ago Delia had been living in the Strand, in the Cape, with her husband and their two Maltese poodles. She had been in the habit of walking the dogs on the beach every evening, and she would stop intermittently to watch the waves crashing against the sandy shore, and wonder at how happy she was, and how blessed. Looking back now, she should have known that something was going to happen to destroy her bliss; she should have recognised the inevitable consequences of acknowledging her good fortune. She often wondered whether God had been jealous of what she had had; if He had been unsatisfied with her simply going to church every Sunday and thanking Him for His blessings. She thought that perhaps God had wanted more and as a result He had struck her husband down so that she would turn to Him instead. Well, it hadn't worked.

Gerald, Delia's husband, had died of a heart attack in their home, in her arms. They had just come back from walking on the beach with the dogs on an unseasonably warm Saturday morning in June. They had stopped off at the Spar on their way home and had bought some croissants for breakfast and a bunch of flowers, because it was the anniversary of the day that they had gone on their first date together, twenty-seven years before. On arriving home, Delia had put the croissants into the oven to warm them up and Gerald had filled the dogs' bowls with cold water. She had decked the two-seater wrought-iron table in their small courtyard with a canary-yellow tablecloth and had set places for her and Gerald. He had brought out the jam and butter, placing them in the centre of the table, and had started grating cheese while she cut the tips off the stems of the flowers they had bought. They had done this all in near silence. Their relationship had been like that from when they first met. They hadn't needed to talk; they seldom had a use for language. Words were superficial to their love. It was for this reason that Delia had always believed, rather naively, that they would die together. How was it possible, after all, that two souls that were so connected, so completely one, could be torn asunder and forced to exist in two separate worlds? This blind faith contributed to the unexpectedness, the absolute impossibility, in Delia's mind, of Gerald's death.

Gerald had been walking to the sink to wash the cheese grater when he had clasped at his chest. It was an odd movement, an almost theatrical movement, but one that had been sudden enough to cause Delia to look up from the flowers she was now arranging in a vase. Within seconds, before Delia could walk across the length of the tiny kitchen of their semi-detached house, Gerald had collapsed onto the floor. Delia had panicked, and panic had frozen her. She hadn't known whether to call the ambulance or to run to her husband, and so she had done neither for a moment. She had simply stared at the flowers that she had dropped onto the floor in her haste. Eventually she had taken the five steps to her husband and had sat down on the floor with him, holding his head in her lap as he breathed his last, gasping breaths. It had taken her a long time to call the ambulance, and when the paramedics arrived the flowers were scattered over the kitchen floor, as if over a grave.

Delia had not known how to live without Gerald. She had forgotten what it was like to be an incomplete soul on earth; how sad and lonely and difficult it was. Eventually her sister and her husband had come to fetch her and had taken her to their home on the San La Mer estate in KwaZulu-Natal. She had been unable to resist; Gerald's death had left her not only emotionally destitute, but also financially insolvent.

Two months after she had moved in with her sister and her husband, they had announced their intention to emigrate to New Zealand. They were leaving in two weeks, they told her. They hadn't wanted to upset her more than she was already, which was why they had not told her sooner. They were, however, planning to keep their house (in case they didn't enjoy New Zealand and wanted to return to their homeland), in which she could stay rent-free for as long as she needed.

Thus it was that Delia found herself grieving the loss of her husband, alone in her sister's house, separated from all her friends and in a foreign province. Although Delia would blame, while she still had the capacity for blame, the snake for her descent into psychosis, the snake was actually just the physical manifestation that came to embody all of Delia's despair.

Delia found the snake one month after her sister's departure. She walked into the kitchen and it was lying curled up around the leg of the kitchen table. Before she could think about what she was doing, Delia screamed. The snake elegantly lifted its lime-green head and looked at her before unravelling itself from the table leg. Delia retraced her steps through the dining room and back up the stairway. By the time she reached the top of the staircase, she was shaking uncontrollably. She was barely able to operate her fingers enough to press the buttons on her cellphone to dial the number of the estate security company.

By the time the security guard arrived, carrying a long forked stick, the snake had slithered out the kitchen door. Delia, who had ventured far enough down the stairs to keep an eye on the snake without coming within its striking range, had watched it make its way leisurely to the door that she had left open earlier in the day. The way the snake moved – the suggestion of muscle beneath its fluid gliding, the tongue constantly flickering in and out, the softest swish as its body zigzagged across the smooth travertine tiles – both fascinated and repelled Delia. She asked the security guard where the snake was likely to have gone, but he merely shrugged his shoulders. This one gesture indicated simultaneously to her that the snake could have gone anywhere, that the guard did not care where it had gone and that Delia's worry was not his concern. His job was done. As he walked out of the door, Delia asked him to close it behind him. She didn't want the snake coming back into the house.

Delia did not think about the snake again until that evening. What concerned her more, initially, was that her conversation with the security guard had been her first with another person since her sister had left. She imagined that it should have felt good to speak to someone other than herself again, but it didn't. She realised that she would be quite happy never to have to speak to anyone again – that there was nothing that anyone could say to her, no conversation that would undo all that had happened over the previous six months – but at the same time, an unwilling part of her understood that this could not be normal. Her sister had left some emergency telephone numbers for Delia and she dialled one of them now.

The receptionist who answered the telephone was abrupt: Have you seen Doctor before? No? Then we can only fit you in next week. Delia wrote the time and date of the appointment on a scrap of paper and left it next to the telephone. She was unsure whether she would keep the appointment or not.

The next time that Delia thought about the snake was that evening, just before she went to bed. She had finished watching television – she had sat through three back-to-back episodes of *Strictly Come Dancing* – and had been walking to the staircase when she thought that she heard the rustle of snake on tiles. She had stopped and listened. The house was quiet but for the creak of the wooden struts contracting in the cool evening air. Nevertheless, she had been convinced that the snake was somewhere in the house. She thought that it must have sneaked in through a window (she had purposely kept the doors closed since the departure of the security guard). She ran upstairs, her heart pounding in her chest, and pulled her bedroom door closed behind her. The window was closed, but there was a chance that the snake had slithered upstairs unnoticed while she was watching television, or earlier in the evening as she was warming up the frozen pasta that she had for supper. She checked beneath her bed, opened the doors of her cupboard and searched the small en suite bathroom. Even though there was no sign of the snake, she could not shake the feeling that it might be hiding somewhere. She slept with the light on that evening.

The following day Delia could not erase the image of the snake from her mind. In her imagination it had grown, doubled in size. She typed 'common Natal snakes' into the Google bar on her phone and, to her horror, concluded that it was probably a green mamba that had made itself comfortable on her floor. In reality, it had been a small, harmless Natal green snake, but Delia managed to convince herself otherwise, imagining that she had seen in her snake all the specific identifying features of a green mamba. Had Delia grown up in KwaZulu-Natal, it is likely that the appearance of the snake would not have bothered her at all. She might even have taken a golf club or a spade to it as it lay on the kitchen floor, and decapitated it before identifying it as a harmless Natal green snake. But Delia had grown up in the Cape and was not used to snakes. They engendered in her a deep, base, almost instinctive repulsion. Of course, her reaction to the snake was also exaggerated by the circumstances in which Delia found herself at the time of her discovery of it.

Over the next few months Delia slowly withdrew into herself. She tricked her mind into believing that she was under attack, so much so that soon the delusion became Delia's entire reality. Initially she sealed the windows, taping them closed with packing tape to ensure that the snake would not find a way into the house. Then one day, after washing some dishes, she had been watching the water drain down the plughole, and she had realised there was the possibility that the snake might come in through one of the drainpipes. Any opening, however narrow or obscure, however well hidden or inaccessible, could serve as a portal of entry. She had gone around the house taping closed all the taps and drains. Used dishes piled up next to the sink and Delia started wearing the same clothes until they were so stiff with dirt that they could no longer be worn. She didn't notice the smell that pervaded the house, that clung to her clammy skin and settled in her hair.

The same fate to which the drainpipes had been doomed had befallen the air-conditioning ducts and ventilation vents. Then one day it had dawned upon Delia that she could seal off rooms. If she made her living area smaller, it would be far easier to keep the snake out. What need had she, a lonely woman with no relatives and no friends, for a house with four bedrooms anyway? She transferred the television into her bedroom, and the kettle. She no longer had any reason to move out of her little room with its en suite bathroom.

During this time, Delia did visit the doctor. She knew, in the light of that tiny wedge of clarity deep beneath the mist that clouded her mind, that she needed help. She would call a taxi to take her to the doctor's rooms and then wait in her bedroom until the taxi hooted outside, before venturing hurriedly through the rest of the house and out of the door to get to the taxi. She never made appointments, for the decision to visit the doctor was always made on the spur of the moment, during those rare, brief recessions when the mist lifted slightly.

Delia would sit and wait in the doctor's waiting room until he was able to squeeze her in between patients who had made prior appointments. The glares of the receptionist floated past her, irrelevant to her neurosis. If the doctor noticed her stink, the filth on her clothes, the picked and raw nail beds, he refrained from commenting. He had, after all, seen far worse. He had done relief work in Gaza, where he had seen men carrying their own traumatically amputated limbs into hospital. He had worked in war-torn Somalia, stitching up the torn vaginas of gang-raped women. For a brief time, he had a practice on the outskirts of a township, where living ghosts riddled with AIDS had populated his rooms. And so, when Delia walked into his consultation office, he did not comment on her appearance. He did not seem to notice the way in which she nervously picked at her cuticles; or her unwashed hair; or the lipstick smeared over the edges of her lips. Perhaps if he had known Delia before her decline – when she washed and straightened her hair daily; when she did weekly home manicures on her nails; and when she could still look other people in the eye – he would have realised the extent of her illness, but because he had never seen her in any other capacity, it never occurred to him that she had ever been otherwise. He was a doctor more comfortable treating physical trauma than mental maladies, and so he simply gave her stronger and stronger tranquillisers at each visit. He kept increasing the dose because Delia complained that she was no better than the last time she saw him. What the doctor did not know, which was something Delia never told him and which he never thought to ask about, was that the tablets were not working, because Delia was not taking them. She would leave the doctor's rooms with the intention of taking the medication, but once she was back in the house, with its reminders of the snake, she would lose her nerve. Initially she had stashed the tablets in the drawer of the dresser at the top of the stairs, but that had become full, and after her most recent visit to the doctor, she had simply left the box of medication lying on top of the dresser. The reason Delia was too scared to take the medication she had been prescribed was that she knew that it would make her sleep – and she could not risk sleeping, because if she did not keep constant vigil the snake would find a way of sneaking into the house.

Delia had seen Tariq Pillay enter her home. From the gap in the curtains of her upstairs window, she had watched him walk furtively to the front door and knock. She had observed him waiting for a response and then, when there was none, pushing open the door. Delia never bothered to lock the door: her fortifications were against a reptile, not against humans. It was more important that she had sealed off the keyhole, stuffing it with toilet paper, than that she lock the door. She heard Tariq walk around the rooms on the lower level and then make his way up the staircase. His approach did not concern her at all. And when he left a few minutes later, her only thought was of whether or not he had closed the front door behind him.

———•—•———

There are so many opportunities, in the build-up to a murder, for it to be prevented. The smallest, most innocent interventions can either hinder or advance the cause of the murderer. There is no option but to believe that our lives are predetermined; that their unfolding is directed by a greater plan. Because how else is it possible to explain how our unconscious choices can have such resounding and often pivotal consequences?

For example, if Tariq had looked up before knocking on the door, he might have seen the slight movement of the curtain or the shadow of a face behind it. He might then have abandoned his plan and instead phoned his supervisor, who might well have sent him home and replaced him with another guard who would not have been asleep at the time of the murder. Alternatively, if Tariq had not been so hasty and had read the name of the medication on the box, which was Valium and not

Panamol, he would not have swallowed the tablets, thereby saving a life and retaining his job. One can play this game of suppositions infinitely: What if Tariq's mother had not hurt herself? What if she had replaced the tablets on Tariq's bedside table? What if Delia had not left the benzodiazepines on the dresser? What if she had responded to Tariq's knocking? But nothing, no analysing with hindsight or postulating alternative hypotheses, can change the course of what actually happened.

Chapter Three

THERE WAS SOMETHING ABOUT the lace corset and matching pair of knickers, other than the exorbitance of the figure on the price tag, that set this lingerie apart as special. Perhaps it was the handworked lace, imported from France, from which it had been crafted that made it exceptional; perhaps it was the ribbon cut from Turkish silk that was threaded through the eyelets of the corset and gathered into a bow perfectly positioned to sit at the base of the wearer's spine, in the middle of the two dimples that delineated the curve between back and bottom; or perhaps it was because each of the delicate freshwater pearls had been specifically selected for their luminosity, and delicately hand-embroidered onto the low-cut neckline. Whatever it was, it seemed almost as though the underwear was destined to play a role in a murder. It was far too conscious of its beauty to remain in the recesses of a cupboard, lying between sheets of soft tissue paper, to be taken out and worn only every now and then for a special occasion.

It may have been that Mr Vernon King sensed something of the danger of its beauty when he bought it, for he hesitated twice during its purchase. His initial trepidation was as he lifted it from the shelf of the exclusive lingerie shop in the Sandton City shopping mall. It was alluringly displayed on the top of a polished walnut dresser, nestled on a sheet of pure white tissue. King touched the lace, tracing his fingers over the pearls and the silk. As he did so, he felt a shiver run from his fingertips to his shoulder. It was more subtle than an electric shock. The only way he could describe the sensation was that his arm had experienced an orgasm, but that was impossible. King withdrew his hand quickly, afraid that if he continued to touch the garment his arousal would become obvious. He was about to move on and would have left behind the beautiful corset and knickers, and the fate they bore, if the shop assistant had not approached him at that very moment.

'Isn't it stunning?' she asked, exhaling as she spoke, as though she was sharing his arousal. Her hair was dark, almost black, pulled into a tight bun at the nape of her neck and her olive eyes were lined in thick black kohl. 'It's the colour,' she said, as though proffering an excuse for her unprofessional lapse. King had not before specifically noticed the colour of the corset. He had seen it in its entirety, had noticed only the completeness of its beauty. Now he examined it more closely. She was right. The colour was unique. It wasn't a common red or an uninviting white or even an elegant black. The colour was somewhere between lilac and turquoise, soft and feminine while at the same time implying a boyish playfulness. It suggested both experience and innocence; confidence and naivety.

'It's a lucky woman you're buying that for. She'll love you for it,' the shop assistant said. King noticed that she never implied that he was buying it for his wife, even though he had seen her glancing at the wedding ring on his left ring finger. She had obviously been trained to be discreet. 'Can I wrap it for you?'

King hesitated for the second time, as though he was aware that in buying the lingerie he would be setting in play a sequence of events over which he would eventually have no control. The assistant mistook his vacillation. 'We can talk about giving you a five per cent discount if you pay cash,' she said.

King was immediately irritated. Price was not a concern. In his irritation he became hasty and forgot his earlier misgivings.

'I'll take it,' he barked.

The assistant folded the lingerie carefully between sheets of tissue and placed it in a glossy black gift bag.

———— ⋅ ————

The underwear was not for King's wife. Firstly, Maddy King would not have fitted into the fine lingerie, even on their wedding day thirty-four years before, when she had been at her most slender. Secondly, Maddy King wore only cotton underwear because she was of the firm belief that anything else led to fungal infections in delicate regions. The Kings had a conservative marriage in which French corsets and knickers did not feature. The questions then arise: For whom was Mr King buying this expensive and exquisitely beautiful lingerie? And how did it come to play a pivotal role in the murder of Advocate Norman Ware?

Vernon and Madeleine King had been married in a traditional Christian ceremony in an Anglican church in the Houghton suburb of Johannesburg. She had been twenty-four and a virgin; he had been twenty-six and had had the occasional casual sexual liaison, none of which had left any lasting impression on him. They had been courting for a year before they were married. It was a union approved of by both sets of parents.

Maddy had completed a bachelor's degree in English literature at the University of the Witwatersrand and was attempting to write an anthology of poetry. She had no serious intention of ever becoming a writer or a poet (her poetry was atrociously sentimental and she insisted on writing only in rhyming couplets), but she needed something to occupy her while she was waiting to meet a husband. King was an accountant for a large mining firm and had repeatedly been told that he had a great career ahead of him.

They met in 1976 at a Sunday afternoon tennis party thrown by a mutual friend. King had noticed Madeleine because she was a formidable tennis player. He had admired her muscular legs, her toned upper body and her strong single-handed backhand and slice serve. Names had been drawn from a hat and they had ended up playing together in the mixed doubles. They had won. And since both of them liked winning, they had decided that they made a good team and that perhaps they should test their compatibility off the court. They were engaged six months later.

King and Maddy both came from money, and for their wedding presents they had received, from her parents, a ten-day trip to the Algarve as well as a portfolio of shares, and from his parents, a new house, fully paid off, in the leafy suburb of Houghton. Four months into their marriage, Maddy fell pregnant with their first child. Over the next twenty years, King progressed up the corporate ladder and Maddy raised three children. Their life was harmonious and seldom disrupted by the unexpected.

Once all the children had completed their schooling and had left for university in the Cape, Maddy and King relocated to Durban, to their holiday home in the San La Mer eco-estate. This was a move they had planned since buying the house five years before. King had not yet fully retired, so he commuted to Johannesburg, working there from a Tuesday morning to a Thursday evening. They had a flat in Killarney, an elegant old apartment with spacious rooms, parquet flooring and pressed ceilings, in which King stayed while he was away from his San La Mer home.

Maddy remained in Durban while King was in Johannesburg. To keep herself busy, she played club tennis three mornings a week, served as the Rotarian secretary and went to Bible-study group on Thursday afternoons. Every Friday King and Maddy would play eighteen holes together and then go for drinks and dinner at the San La Mer clubhouse.

Many people would find it difficult not to mock the suburban nature of King and Maddy's union. They might find it quaint that she had married as a virgin and had only ever slept with her husband; they could think the club tennis and the Friday golf predictable, or even self-absorbed, and suggest instead that Maddy should spend her time doing something more philanthropic; they might even condemn the union as banal and habitual, doomed to failure. But the truth was that King and Maddy were content, if not happy. The life they led was what they had imagined when they stood together in front of the priest and made their vows to each other. It was the same predictable, conventional life that their parents had led and that they wished for their children. Until Mr King began his affairs, neither he nor Maddy was aware of any dissatisfaction with their marital arrangement.

The one crack in their relationship, and it was a weakness that Maddy largely chose to ignore, related to their sex life. When King and Maddy were first married, they had had sexual intercourse at least three times a week. Although Maddy did not particularly enjoy sex or understand the reason for having it, apart from procreation, she appreciated that it was expected of her, as a wife, that she have sex with her husband, and so, on a Tuesday, a Friday and a Saturday evening, she would dutifully turn off the lights, lie on her back and allow her husband to penetrate her. Sex was a duty that Maddy performed without complaint, but it was a duty nonetheless, classed with cleaning the car or doing the ironing. After the birth of their first child, the rate of their sexual intercourse dwindled to a twice-weekly event, and after their second child came, they were having sex only every now and then. This was not entirely Maddy's fault. King was busy at work and his hours were long, so there was not always time, between his work and Maddy's breastfeeding and caring for the children, to make love. On top of this, King decided at this stage that he wanted to run the Comrades Marathon, the training for which left him too exhausted for lovemaking most Saturday and Sunday nights (he did his long runs on these days). Naturally Maddy supported her husband fully in his attempt to run the Comrades, and when he decided that he wanted to do it again the following year and aim for a Bill Rowan medal, she continued to support him. By the time their youngest child was three, King and Maddy went for long stretches, sometimes for months, without making love.

Maddy did not see their paucity of sexual intercourse as a problem. Firstly, she did not miss the sex and so she simply presumed that her husband did not miss it either. She had grown up in an era in which sex was not spoken about, so she never thought to ask him. Secondly, Maddy, who was naturally a large-boned woman, had put on a lot of weight with the birth of her children and had become self-conscious about her body, which made sex awkward. Thirdly, their relationship was not lacking in love or affection, which made it difficult for Maddy to see that there was indeed a problem. It was enough for her that she and her husband were steadfast friends.

King, on the other hand, missed having sex. He had tried to tell this to Maddy on numerous occasions, but because he was too well bred to blurt it out, she was able to ignore or misinterpret his attempts at raising the subject. This left King in a difficult predicament. He loved and respected his wife too much to cheat on her, either with a prostitute or by having a traditional affair, but at the same time he had certain carnal needs that had to be fulfilled. He had not, after all, signed up for a life of celibacy.

Initially, he managed to control his urges by masturbating. Once that was no longer enough, he went online and bought some adult DVDs. The whole process was a lot easier than he had imagined and far less embarrassing, since the internet interface saved him from any face-to-face contact. At first, the pornography worked well in assuaging his urges, but after some time that too fell flat. He tried phone sex and blow-up dolls, also ordered via an adult website, but soon realised there was something more that he was missing: it was the deeply intimate physical contact with another human being that only sexual intercourse provides that he really desired. It was while he was watching one of his adult DVDs one evening that it occurred to him that there was a way in which he would be able to have sex while not actually, in his mind, cheating on his wife. The blue movie that he was watching was a threesome between one woman and two men, and was probably more explicit than King usually liked; however, on this particular evening he found himself very aroused. Strangely, it was the display of the two men together that turned him on. It was then that King decided that if he cheated on his wife with another man as opposed to another woman, it could not really be considered a betrayal of their marriage vows. At the same time, because he was happily married, he would not be obliged to label himself as homosexual. King suffered from a socially conditioned aversion to homosexuality that was not uncommon among his peer group.

His logic, of course, was flawed. Desire had muddled his thoughts in the same way that an anorexic becomes obsessed with recipes and believes that by chewing his or her food and then spitting it out, or merely by inhaling the aroma of food, he or she is eating. But King, starved of intimate sexual contact for six years, was unable to recognise the perversity of his reasoning.

It was easy to find a male escort agency online. King chose the most expensive one, once again using faulty logic to convince himself that if the experience was expensive, it was somehow less cheap. He prepared for the evening by buying condoms. He chose the feather-thin ones that promised maximum sensation for him and her, although it was only his own pleasure that King was particularly concerned about. The escort (King subconsciously refused to use the word *prostitute*) who arrived at King's Johannesburg flat was an average-looking man in his mid-twenties. King scrutinised him as he ushered him into the lobby: he could be someone that King walked past at the gym or sat beside at a rugby game. There was nothing about the man that made him stand out as a male prostitute, no aberration of clothing or grooming. This relaxed King a little. If Maddy popped in – he knew she wouldn't because she was in Durban, but if, hypothetically, she did – King would be able to pass the man off as a business associate. The act itself, the betrayal, took all of fifteen minutes.

Over time, King refined his tastes. He learnt to request certain types of men from the agency: he preferred small-framed, more effeminate men, and if possible, he chose blonds over brunettes. He came to enjoy the power that paying for carnal pleasure bestowed on him: that he could choose exactly when and where (within the confines of Johannesburg) and how sex took place. After years and years of having to plead in nuances; of having tender advances rejected – a hand brusquely pushed away from a thigh or breast, or lips drawn closed against his hesitantly probing tongue – of having to plan and hope and humble himself, it felt liberating to demand. His Tuesday and Wednesday evening liaisons changed him. They gave him something to look forward to, something to excite and titillate him during his days at work. He developed a new energy that permeated all aspects of his life. He restructured the financial department of the company for which he worked and his golf handicap improved by two strokes. He started training at the gym, rediscovering muscles that had last been visible in his Comrades-running days. If Maddy noticed a change in him when he came home on a Thursday evening, she either failed to or chose not to comment on it.

King kept his extramarital activities strictly confined

to Johannesburg, and his and Maddy's joint life in Durban continued as it always had. Soon the Tuesday and Wednesday rendezvous became another routine in King's rigidly organised life. King managed to continue to delude himself that he was doing his wife no wrong by sleeping with men. He believed his deception so completely that when colleagues or associates mentioned affairs or one-night flings at the bar after work, he found his fellow workers distasteful, and smugly congratulated himself that he had not fallen so foul of the straight and narrow.

This state of affairs, or misaffairs, could have continued indefinitely had King not decided one morning to take an inexcusable risk and have sex with a man in his home in San La Mer. King was on leave from work for a week and woke up on the morning of the second of November feeling overwhelmingly horny. He should have quelled his urge by masturbating, but perhaps he was subconsciously seeking a greater thrill. King knew the cause of his desire: it was the lingerie that he had bought on impulse from a boutique in Sandton City the previous Thursday after work. The contents of the glossy bag, which he had locked away in the drawer of his desk at home and which he meant to take back with him when he returned to Johannesburg after his week of leave, taunted him day and night. King had recently discovered immeasurable pleasure in ordering his escorts to dress up in women's lingerie and parade themselves before him prior to stripping for him, and he was impatient to experiment with his recent purchase. As with any forbidden fruit, the more King tried to ignore the lingerie that he had bought, the more tempting it became to him.

Maddy had left early for tennis – she played second division ladies league on a Wednesday and King knew she would be away until at least two o'clock, because the match was against a club on the South Coast – so King had the house to himself for the morning. He went online to see if the escort agency that he usually used had a branch in Durban. As luck, or fate, would have it, it did. King dialled the number listed on the website and requested an escort for the morning.

The escort arrived forty-five minutes after King had made the phone call and King led him upstairs to the main bedroom, where he had laid the lingerie out artistically on the king-size bed.

Had King not been so mesmerised by the vision of the lilac-turquoise lace corset and matching knickers on the slight but well-toned male prostitute, he might have noticed the rain. It was a gentle drizzle over the San La Mer estate, but ninety kilometres south, it was pounding down in relentless sheets of water, flooding the tennis courts of the Amanzimtoti tennis club and preventing the ladies league players from continuing with their match. The storm was being driven north by an angry wind and Maddy raced the bad weather home, arriving at the San La Mer estate a good hour before the squall would.

At the very moment that Maddy pushed the button on the remote control that opened the garage door, King was in the master bedroom kneeling naked behind his escort, rubbing himself against the lace of the new lingerie. Had it not been for the squeak of the automated garage door rolling up, Maddy would have walked in on her husband penetrating a male prostitute. As it was, the noise of the slightly rusty garage door did not alert King, who was in the blissful throes of near orgasm, but the escort, who was adept at listening out for such noises. He brought King's raptures to an abrupt halt as he tore the underwear from his body and quickly dressed himself. He had the presence of mind to run to King's study, where King, dressed in an unusually dishevelled manner, met him just a couple of seconds before Maddy walked into the house.

Maddy, hearing male voices in the study and presuming that her husband was having a business meeting, went to the kitchen to make herself a cup of tea without greeting King. She caught a brief glimpse of the man she believed to be her husband's colleague – enough to notice his slight build and sandy hair and spectacles – as King escorted him to the door a few minutes later. Maddy stopped her husband on his way back to the study and offered him a cup of tea. King, whose stomach now felt like a washing machine on the spin cycle, declined. It was only when Maddy mentioned that she was going upstairs to have a shower that King remembered the underwear that had been thrown down on their bedroom floor. He pushed himself past Maddy and raced upstairs to the bedroom. In his panic, the only thing that he could think of doing to dispose of the evidence was to throw the expensive underwear out of the window, after which he ran to the toilet and proceeded to disgorge the contents of his intestines into the porcelain bowl. When Maddy reached the bedroom, King was sitting hunched over on the toilet in the throes of severe abdominal cramping. Maddy attributed his odd behaviour to a stomach bug and went down the hall to the medicine cabinet, where she kept the Imodium, to fetch a tablet for her husband.

It was as King was sitting on the toilet amidst the stench of diarrhoea, while his wife was hunting in the medicine chest for medication for him, that his self-delusion was shattered. He was faced with the undeniable, inexcusable truth that he had cheated on his wife and that he had very narrowly missed screwing everything up. It was purely through luck, and the experience of the prostitute, that Maddy had not discovered him in the act of fornication.

There is always the possibility, the hope, that after an epiphany of this sort, the offending incident can be left behind and that life can be resumed as it was before the sequence of events leading up to the revelation was set in motion. Certainly King shared this hope. He felt adequately chastened and berated. The effects of his near-exposure experience had been similar to those of a near-death experience: he felt as though he was reborn; as though he had been given a new lease on life, a second chance. He was brimming over with both resolve and good resolutions. Unfortunately, he had not taken into account the natural law of action and consequence. His feelings of remorse could no more change the effects of his chosen course of action than wishing to be weightless could alter the law of gravity.

The results of King's illicit liaisons were not immediately obvious. He did not have to spend the rest of his life paying off a sandy-haired short-term insurance broker for his silence; there were no sordid photographs splashed across the front page of the local newspaper; and Maddy never discovered the secret life that King had led. Instead, once the initial glow of redemption had settled, King began to feel dissatisfied. He wanted the comfort and safety of his life with Maddy, that simplicity that he had so narrowly avoided destroying, but at the same time he missed the frisson of excitement that his affairs had provided. King was caught in a state of inertia, greedily guarding the life that he had almost lost and yet yearning for the allure of the forbidden. As the years passed, he became more and more dissatisfied. Bitterness grew inside him and began to deform his joints, leaving them as twisted and damaged as his mind. Guilt and self-disgust racked him. King was doomed, his fate sealed by the actions of his past. He would live a long life, but the burden of his lies, betrayed only by the deformity of his joints, would remain with him, negating any chance of happiness.

King's actions on that morning of the second of November had other consequences, consequences of which he was completely unaware and which would play an important role in the murder of Advocate Norman Ware. The corset and knickers that he had so anxiously and myopically thrown out of the window had floated softly downwards, not completely oblivious to their own significance. They eventually came to rest on the washing line of the Kings' neighbours, where they settled themselves neatly between a pair of grey woollen trousers and a collared Polo shirt. And when the storm arrived at San La Mer an hour later, in a howl of wind and rain, they had been hastily gathered in with the rest of the washing on the line. They were ready to play out their destiny.

Chapter Four

To what extent is a person accountable for the consequences of his or her actions? Does the onus of responsibility end with the direct outcome of an action, or does answerability continue indefinitely, to the point at which the original action is entirely forgotten, traceable only through a careful dissection of the trail of indirect consequences that led up to it? This is a philosophical debate and one might argue that it has little relevance to the practicalities of daily life, but one has to consider it when attempting to understand the role that Dumazile, a trader in body parts, played in Advocate Norman Ware's murder and the events that followed it.

Dumazile Dlamini's mother had cried on her daughter's birth. They were not tears of joy, an overflow of happiness at the beginning of a new life, but tears of disappointment shed at both the gender and the appearance of the child that had slipped from her womb. Thembi, who already had six daughters, had convinced herself that this, her seventh child, would be the boy that her heart so dearly desired. Twice during her pregnancy, she had gone to Busisiwe, who was able to look into the stomachs of pregnant mothers and tell whether they were carrying a boy child or a girl child, and both times Busisiwe had reassured her that the baby inside her was a boy child. How could Busisiwe, who had never been wrong in fifty years, make a mistake? The only answer that made sense to Thembi was that there was witchcraft involved. Her mind wandered to those who might want to curse her. She thought of her neighbour, Pearl, who was barren, unable to carry a child in her womb. Perhaps she had been jealous of Thembi, who had borne six children and was now carrying her seventh. Perhaps it had been the spiteful wife of her brother who had put a spell on her, or the drunk who hung around outside the spaza shop and whom Thembi had cursed many times. Whoever it was who had put a spell on her, there was no doubt in Thembi's mind that there had been sorcery involved, for how else could she have given birth to a child who was both a girl and a witch?

Dumazile had been born with a deep-purple birthmark marring one side of her face, and although her mother firmly believed otherwise, it was not the result of witchcraft but rather an aberration of the blood vessels that had caused them to become swollen and engorged and had left them visible beneath the skin. It could easily have been treated with laser, but neither Thembi nor her daughter knew that, so Dumazile would grow up trying to hide the deformity that made adults spit and children taunt when she walked past. There is a chance that Dumazile had been born with an evil heart, as her mother believed, and that she had been destined to become a witch, but it is far more likely that she had had no other choice. Hers was a fate shaped by default, not choice; the result of self-preservation in a society that places too much importance on appearance.

From the moment that her mother's salty tears fell

onto her sticky, vernix-coated body, Dumazile had been doomed to unhappiness. Thembi had tried once to put Dumazile to her breast, but the sight of the ugly purple blemish against the skin of her chest repulsed Thembi and she had torn her child from her bosom in horror. Dumazile had already been forsaken before she had been out of her mother's womb for twenty-four hours. Thembi's mother, Dumazile's grandmother, had fed Dumazile with a bottle filled with diluted goat's milk and had washed the infant and held her, while Thembi sobbed. And when they left the hospital – Dumazile, her mother and her grandmother – it had been her grandmother who carried the tiny Dumazile.

For the first five years of her life, Dumazile had been protected to some degree by her grandmother. The old lady had chased away the children who would come to throw stones at the toddler, and had shouted at the whispering or snickering adults. Dumazile's grandmother fed Dumazile and braided her hair and sang to her at night. Then, on the day that Dumazile turned five, her grandmother had not woken up. Dumazile had found her lying on her mattress on the floor, her body stiff and crumpled on one side. Dumazile had fled from the hut and had hidden herself in an old, eroded anthill outside the village, where she allowed the tears to stream down her unmatched cheeks. Even though she had not yet lost her first milk tooth, she knew that with her grandmother's death she had been forsaken once again, this time completely.

―――

Dumazile had been forced to learn to survive. She had become a scavenger, picking up the scraps of food thrown away after other people's meals. She had slept outside with the dogs, stealing their heat. The dogs had not minded. Perhaps they had seen her as one of themselves: scrawny, unwashed, beaten and used. Then one day Dumazile had had a seizure. It was linked to her birthmark. In the same way that some of the blood vessels on her face were overgrown, some of the vessels in her cerebral vasculature were enlarged and this blood vessel tumour had begun to squash part of her brain, triggering a grand mal convulsion. Of course, none of the villagers ascribed Dumazile's seizure to epilepsy. It was obvious to them that it was witchcraft. Certain of the villagers thought that Dumazile should be chased away, out of the village, but others were too scared now to risk offending her in any way. Dumazile's seizure had shifted her position in the social hierarchy. She was still as disliked as before, but as a result of her perceived association with evil, people had begun to fear her too.

It did not take Dumazile long to manipulate the potential of her situation. She came to understand that when the smell of oranges filled her nose, she was going to have a convulsion, and she would make sure that she was publicly visible. Each time that she recovered from a fit, with bloodstained saliva smeared on her face and urine soaking her tattered clothes, people's fear grew and, with it, her power. Children stopped throwing stones at her and cowered instead when she passed. Pregnant women averted their gaze when their paths crossed hers, in case she should curse their unborn children. She no longer had to survive on scraps: staring at an adult who was eating would cause the person to discard the barely touched meal. Soon Dumazile moved back, uninvited, to her mother's place. It was not because she particularly wanted to live with her family – she was happy with the dogs – but because she wanted to test the measure of her influence. Within a week, her mother and siblings had gone to live elsewhere, leaving her alone in the family hut.

One day, when Dumazile was sixteen, a woman approached her. It had been at dusk, at the time of ghosts, when people and shadows merged, and Dumazile had known instinctively that the woman had chosen that time to come to her because she had not wanted to be seen. Dumazile had taken her inside her hut and the woman had handed her a small beaded bag filled with coins. The woman's hand was shaking as she held the money out. Dumazile recognised the woman, and because she spent most of her time watching the people around her, she knew why the woman had come. Dumazile had noticed certain glances between this woman and a man who was not her husband. She had seen them brush hands. She had watched the woman walk down the dusty red road that led from the village and then seen the man follow, a few minutes later. She also knew that the woman's husband was working in Durban and had not been home for three months, and that he still sent her money every month, which she collected from the post office, so he was not yet living with another woman. Dumazile had noticed how this woman who was standing in front of her had become fatter over the past few months and how her breasts had become full and pendulous.

Before the woman had had a chance to open her mouth, Dumazile had spoken what she knew. The woman's hand began to shake even more. Dumazile took the money and sent the woman away.

The next morning, as the sun was stealing the silver dew from the grass, Dumazile walked down the red road and picked the leaves of certain plants. She placed the collected leaves into a plastic packet, along with a dead gecko that had been squashed by a passing car. Once she got home, she crushed the leaves and the gecko between two flat stones and then put the mixture in a pot of water, which she left boiling on the Primus stove until it became thick and dark. She decanted this concoction into a cup and gave it to the woman to drink. Within hours of drinking the muti, the woman had begun to vomit. Soon her stomach started to cramp, and by the next morning she had expelled dark red clots of foetus.

Dumazile had not been trained as a sangoma or herbalist. She had picked the leaves randomly, choosing those that looked ugly or smelt strong. It may have been that by chance she had picked the leaves of a plant that had the capacity to induce an abortion, or that the mixture Dumazile had given the woman had poisoned her system and thereby brought about the miscarriage. It is equally possible that the woman was going to have a miscarriage anyway and that Dumazile had been lucky with her timing. Whichever was the case, the incident opened the door of possibility for Dumazile. She realised the potential for wealth that her deformity held. With time, she herself started to believe that she had supernatural powers, that she was untouchable.

Over the next ten years Dumazile upscaled her business and her lifestyle. She moved from the small village of her birth to the town of Stanger, an hour north of Durban. Her client base grew through word of mouth, and before long she was earning enough to rent a room on the main road, above a wholesale grocer. She had flyers printed advertising her services, which she gave to a man to hand out at traffic lights in exchange for the assurance that she would make his wife return to him. On the flyers, she called herself Mama Doctor. She saw her clients in her room above the wholesaler, with the curtains drawn and the odour of rotten vegetables seeping in through the broken windowpane.

Dumazile soon figured out which services brought in the highest revenue and began to specialise in these. She listed them on her flyers:

Making penis bigger and staying hard for longer
Permanent Cure of HIV AIDS
Problems with Bad Debt
Problems with people putting Spells or Bad Luck on
you
Winning Lotto
Problems with gambling or with wife not being
faithful

She continued to ensure that her seizures occurred in public; that whenever she started to smell oranges, she grabbed some of her flyers and ran downstairs into the street or the shop, where people would be offered visual proof of her authenticity. She was unable to differentiate the smell of real oranges from the hallucinatory aroma of her auras, and in winter, more than once, she ran downstairs expecting to start convulsing but instead finding a delivery truck offloading citrus fruit to the wholesaler. On occasion she was taken to hospital after having had a convulsion and, after being stabilised, was given medication by the doctors: little packets of white tablets to take twice a day to keep the seizures at bay. She never took them, nor did she keep the follow-up appointments that were booked for her. She knew that her fits raised her above the level of other witchdoctors, singled her out as bona fide.

Instead of ingesting the tablets that the doctors prescribed for her, she ground them up and added them to the bottles of muti she sold. Her customers appeared to like it when the medicine she gave them made them feel a little odd or spaced out. It seemed that it was proof to them that her potions were efficacious. It was once Dumazile had realised this that she hit upon the idea of sourcing more interesting ingredients than roadside herbs, domestic cleaning agents and the occasional crushed anti-epileptic tablet for her potions. She had inadvertently stumbled across the charlatan's truth, the same truth that had shaped her destiny: appearance holds far more weight than reality.

It was easy for Dumazile to get a regular supply of anti-epileptics from the hospital, so her concoctions all had differing concentrations of Phenytoin or Tegretol in them. It did not take her long to add depression and anxiety to her own repertoire of illnesses. The symptoms were, after all, so easy to fake and she was already visiting the hospital once a month for the management of her epilepsy. She found that the antidepressants and sedatives that the overworked doctors gave her without question were even more effective in her potions than the anti-epileptics. Dumazile made it known in the long queue outside the hospital pharmacy that she was willing to buy patients' medication off them for twenty rands, and soon she added antihypertensives, antibiotics, oral hyperglycaemic agents and diuretics to her muti.

In keeping with the new philosophy driving her business, Dumazile redecorated her room. She hung bunches of dried herbs from the ceiling and paid local children to bring her dead geckos and snakeskins, which she laid out on shelves or piled up in woven grass baskets. The room began to stink of death, but that did not pose a problem for Dumazile. She was used to the smell of decay. Besides, it made her clients eager to leave more quickly, which suited her. Dumazile upped her price to two hundred rands for a consultation, not including the cost of the muti that she dispensed. She would adjust the price of her medication according to how desperate she gauged her clients to be. The more fraught they were, the more she would charge them for their potions. Her cure for AIDS usually proved to be her most expensive muti. Dying people were, after all, the most desperate.

Dumazile began to live a double life. After hours she resided in a middle-class suburb in a neat semi-detached house that she rented, and she drove a Golf GTI. She wore clothes from the more expensive chain stores and bought her meals from Woolworths. During the day she dressed herself in rags and animal skins, which she kept stored in a small chest in her consultation room, and waited for clients in the darkness of her hovel above the wholesaler. All of her transactions were cash only. Criminals were too afraid of her power to hassle her, and her clients never had the courage to complain to her if the treatments she sold them did not work.

For the first time, Dumazile was experiencing happiness in her life. She had no qualms about lying to her clients. If they were stupid enough to convince themselves that she could cure their HIV or make their penis larger, or so weak-willed that they were unable to stop their gambling or drinking without a stranger's help, she believed that they deserved to be deceived. She had no sympathy for people who relied on quick fixes for problems that they themselves had created. She had suffered and worked hard to get what she had. She had been forced to develop wiliness and cunning, to learn to read people's behaviour, to watch her every step. There had been no quick fixes in her life. And so Dumazile had little time for others' weaknesses. They were there to be exploited by those who were stronger.

There was, however, one aspect to her job that did plague her conscience. Occasionally, she had clients who demanded either that she sell them dried human appendages as tokens or charms or that their muti contain human body parts or organs. She charged far more for these potions, sometimes prices in the thousands, both because the body parts were expensive to procure and because such transactions unsettled her. Dumazile did not harvest the body parts herself. She had two people from whom she bought these items, but she tried to have as little to do with them as possible. She was a charlatan, a quack, but she did not consider herself a murderer. Perhaps there was the lingering, subconscious knowledge that had circumstances been different, her mother might well have sold her off to one of these body harvesters. She would have been the perfect candidate.

Chapter Five

ALONG WITH HER FATHER's infrequent visits, one of the things that six-year-old Emily looked most forward to in life was visiting her horse. She didn't enjoy riding the horse very much, because she was a little afraid of heights and she felt very high up on the back of Beauty, but she loved standing on the wooden stepladder to brush Beauty's mane and stroke her velvety coat, and holding her hand out flat to allow Beauty to eat the apples and carrots that she brought with her. Beauty was almost the same colour as an almond, but she was shinier, as though someone had spent a long time polishing the almond. Emily's father called her chestnut, but this made little sense to Emily since she had never seen a chestnut, and she preferred to describe the colour of her horse as polished almond.

Sadly, young Emily did not very often get the chance to visit her horse. Her mother seldom took her, because she disliked the muddy stables and complained about the flies and the smell and the rude stable attendants, and her father, who loved horses as much as she did, and who also had a horse in the stables, named Firefly, was seldom at home. Which was why Emily was so excited when her mother promised her on the way to school on the morning of the second of November that she would take her to the stables to visit Beauty that afternoon.

The stables that Emily looked so forward to visiting, and that her mother disliked so intensely, were on the San La Mer estate. They had been built by some of the horse-loving residents so that they would no longer have to traipse all the way out to Shongweni when they wanted to ride their noble steeds. Instead, the horses were housed on an enclosure within the small area of protected forest on the estate, where stables and a paddock had been built for them. The incongruity of having stables situated within the last acre of properly preserved coastal forest on the North Coast was not lost on all the residents of San La Mer, and there were ongoing battles between the horse-lovers and the eco-activists. Petitions were continually being sent out and signed by the various factions. Court cases were held and thrown out and bribes were paid. In the meantime, while the arguing continued, the horses were safe and Emily and her father were happy.

———❖———

Cherise Andreakos had promised her daughter a trip to the stables because she was feeling guilty. This was the manner in which she usually assuaged her guilt when it became too intrusive for her to ignore. Going to the stables, although it disgusted Cherise, was an easy and relatively thoughtless way in which to make Emily happy. And making Emily happy while performing an act of self-sacrifice, even though it was only her expensive grooming and exaggerated sense of femininity that she was sacrificing, allowed Cherise to convince herself that she was not actually so atrocious a mother.

Cherise had had Emily against her wishes. She

was twenty-six when she had discovered that she was pregnant. She had gone to the doctor because she had been feeling nauseous and bloated and depressed and convinced herself, after having read in a popular magazine about a celebrity who had gained twenty kilograms after her thyroid had stopped working properly, that she had developed an underactive thyroid. Cherise had listed her symptoms to the doctor, and before even examining her thyroid, the doctor had done a pregnancy test on her.

Cherise had not considered that she might be pregnant, because she was on an oral contraceptive, so the news had come to her as a horrible and very unwelcome shock. She had made the doctor do a blood test and an ultrasound scan before she was convinced that she was carrying a child and that her thyroid was actually functioning normally. Later that afternoon, drunk and in tears, she had told her husband she was pregnant, and his reaction had alternated between ecstasy and fury. He had hugged her and then, almost immediately after releasing her, shouted at her for drinking; he had tenderly felt her stomach and then rushed to pour the remainder of the bottle of champagne down the drain with such an expression of disgust on his face that he looked almost deformed; he had phoned his brother with the news, crying tears of joy, and then flung the empty bottle onto the floor, where it had shattered into dozens of glittering green shards. It was the first time that her husband had shown Cherise any anger, and she was more upset by the fact that he was so indifferent to her feelings that he was able to show his own displeasure than by the actual emotion itself. Cherise was acutely aware, even in her drunken state, of a shift in the dynamics of their relationship. She had been displaced by the unborn bean inside her. She, who up to this point had been able to manipulate her husband, to play him like a marionette, was being forced to listen to a list of rules that he was shouting at her: no more drinking, no more smoking, start behaving like an adult, no drugs, eat properly, go to bed early. Because she was now carrying her husband's child, it was as though he had claimed some ill-defined right to the choices she made concerning her body. Her individuality had been diluted by her husband's DNA.

As the pregnancy progressed, the shift in the balance of power became more and more pronounced. Cherise convinced herself that her husband had swapped her oral contraceptive with a placebo in an attempt to make her pregnant, so that he could more easily control and subjugate her. Her husband was, in fact, innocent of such deceit, and it was more likely to have been one of the numerous pills that Cherise had forgotten to take or had taken late that contributed to her falling pregnant. Nevertheless, after Emily's birth, Cherise had an intrauterine contraceptive device inserted to ensure that her husband would not be able to play the same cruel trick on her a second time.

In utero, Emily had been nothing but a burden to her mother. Cherise's lifestyle was not conducive to pregnancy and her husband's threats had not been idle. He had started policing her, punishing her every time she dared to touch alcohol or cigarettes. A glass of champagne might result in the closure of her account at an exclusive fashion boutique, while just a few cigarettes could prompt the confiscation of a favourite piece of jewellery. The penal measures were pecuniary because that was the lever with which their unequal marriage had provided him. She had contributed her youth, beauty and sex appeal; he, his money. When Mr Andreakos was not at home, which was often because his work as one of the directors of an international investment consortium took him all over the world, he got one of the domestic workers to spy on Cherise and report back to him.

To Cherise's credit, she never once blamed the tiny foetus inside her for the changes for which her pregnancy had acted as a catalyst. Cherise was a bad mother because she was self-centred, emotionally immature and narcissistic, not because she resented her child. Her anger was all towards her husband. She enacted her fury in small but potent measures: withholding sex from her husband; refusing to answer his telephone calls; faking problems with the pregnancy (she managed to get herself admitted to hospital at least half a dozen times during her confinement, all while he was away). By the time that Emily was born, her parents were hardly speaking to each other.

Over the next few years, Cherise and her husband reached a volatile truce. He expected her to play out the role she had signed up for: to bedazzle at his side; to laugh at his jokes and gaze at him adoringly; to make herself carnally available to him. He, in turn, was liable for subsidising her expensive habits and tastes. Their marriage had been stripped down to its essence: a financial transaction. So where did this leave their innocent and unsuspecting child?

Emily became used to receiving intermittent doses of love from her parents. During the brief periods when her father was home, he spoilt her excessively. While he was away, she heard nothing from him. Cherise's affection towards Emily was erratic and unstable. She would do irrational things such as waking Emily up at one o'clock in the morning on a school night, after having come home from a party, and insisting on having a midnight feast of chocolate and condensed milk with Emily. Or she would take Emily with her to the beauty salon and get the therapist to put gel nail polish on her nails and pluck her eyebrows and give her a massage. Emily pretended to like these outings because she was so desperate for her mother's affection, but in truth she dreaded them. They held little interest for her and she struggled to understand the gossip between her mother and the beauty therapist. Whenever she questioned them about things that she didn't understand, they would wink at each other and laugh loudly as though she had made a joke. Their mock hilarity would leave her feeling embarrassed and angry. And the following day she would get into trouble at school for wearing nail polish. She was too shy to explain the situation to her teacher, so she became adept at chipping the gel off her fingernails with a kitchen knife.

There was not much that was constant in Emily's life. Cherise would often sleep late and forget to take Emily to school, so Emily had little routine. It was only when her father was home that she went to school every day. Meals were erratic: she might have leftover sushi one night, peanut butter sandwiches the following three nights, and then a litre of chocolate custard on the fifth night. No one measured the nutritional content of her food or monitored her fruit and vegetable intake. She was simply fed, by the housekeeper, with whatever was available.

In order to deal with the instability and inconsistency of her life, Emily made up an alternative reality for herself. She imagined that she had a mother like that of her friend, Tatum, and that she lived in a house like Tatum's.

Tatum's mother wore tracksuit pants and T-shirts

most of the time and her nails were often dirty because she loved gardening. She kissed Tatum goodbye and told her that she loved her each morning when she dropped her off outside the classroom and gave Tatum a hug when she fetched her from school in the afternoons. Emily had often gone to play at Tatum's house. Tatum's mother would give them cheese-and-ham sandwiches and sliced pieces of apple after school, which they would eat at a little blue plastic table in a room called the family room. After lunch they would help Tatum's mother bake cupcakes or biscuits, which they would decorate with tiny icing-sugar dolphins or stars, or chocolate ants. Then they would play in Tatum's room, which she shared with her baby brother. If either of them fell and hurt herself during the afternoon, Tatum's mother would rub special cream onto the injury and stick on a Barbie plaster. Sometimes Emily pretended to fall just so that she could get the special ointment and the plaster. When Tatum's mom dropped Emily back at her home in the evening, she would always hug Emily goodbye and give Emily some of the cupcakes or biscuits they had baked earlier in the day. Tatum had once told Emily that she was not allowed to play at Emily's house. Emily was glad; she far preferred going to Tatum's house. She never questioned the arrangement, because she was worried that if she did, the visits to Tatum's house would end.

In her imaginary life, besides having a mother like Tatum's mother, Emily had twelve brothers, all of whom were older than she. They would play with her while her mother was asleep on the couch in the afternoons. They would come to school with her and explain to the teacher why she had not brought the empty egg box or old sock or whatever else it was that she was supposed to bring with her to school, or why she had packed her gym clothes on the day that she was supposed to pack her swimming togs. Sometimes they would even pack her school bag for her. The only problem with her brothers was that they insisted on watching her get changed, so she devised a way to change into her pyjamas without exposing her body.

If Emily had ever been taken to a child psychologist, and he or she had been allowed a glimpse into Emily's imaginary life, it would have been a matter of concern that, even in her ideal life, Emily's father was absent most of the time.

Since Emily spent a large proportion of her time in an imaginary life, she came across as a very shy, introverted little girl. Her teachers often wondered whether she was slightly autistic. They bandied about terms like 'Asperger's' and 'autistic spectrum' without fully understanding what they meant. Perhaps they attributed some of the aspects of her behaviour that baffled them, such as her constant thumb sucking and hair twirling, or the way that she stared out of the classroom window for hours, to this. It was odd that Emily's teachers never realised the full extent of her neglect. This was partially the fault of the housekeeper, who did what she could to ensure that Emily went to school with her face washed and her hair brushed and with polony sandwiches in her lunch box, and partially their own fault. The teachers at Emily's private school were all very well aware of the mini-celebrity status of Emily's mother: the fact that she had been a finalist in the Miss South Africa beauty pageant and that she had once featured in *FHM*'s sexiest hundred women; that pictures of her were routinely splashed across the social pages of local newspapers and magazines; and that she had filled in her occupation on the school application form as 'model and personality'. Cherise's persona allowed her a certain amount of leeway that would not be given to any other, more ordinary, tracksuit-donning mother. It is also possible that the teachers were a little blinded by their own preconceived ideas. If they had been teaching at a public school in the middle of a township, they might well have picked up the neglect and immediately referred Emily to a social worker. But they were not working in a poor school. They were teaching at an exclusive private school and Emily came from a family who made frequent donations of large sums of money to the school fund. It was almost incomprehensible to them that wealth and neglect could coexist.

———◆———

Emily spent most of the morning of Wednesday the second of November imagining the promised visit to Beauty. If they had been quizzed, her teachers might have commented that Emily was, on that morning, more distracted than usual; that they had to prompt her at least three times before she would follow a command; that she didn't show her usual interest in playing with her friend Tatum. In Emily's mind, this visit to the stables was going to be different from, and better than, any of her previous visits. It was going to be a visit that would fulfil her every expectation. To that end, she planned it to the minutest detail.

She would make her mother stop at Woolworths on the way home from school to buy Beauty's favourite foods: apples and carrots. Emily would choose the apples herself because she knew that Beauty preferred the firm, shiny, dark red ones. When they got home, Emily would get changed into her riding clothes. Even though she had no intention of mounting Beauty, she liked wearing the cream jodhpurs and the blue velvet shirt with little bow-shaped buttons and the neat brown patent-leather boots that her father had bought her. The clothes made her feel as though she was meant to be at the stables; that she was a regular there, and not just an infrequent visitor. She imagined that the stable attendants approved of her wearing her riding clothes when she visited Beauty, and that was important to her because she could see how much they disliked her mother.

As soon as Emily was dressed, she and her mother would get into the golf cart and drive down the hill and across the bridge and through the forest to get to the stables. Usually Cherise would remain seated in the golf cart, thumbs frantically flying across the keypad of her BlackBerry, while Emily went to brush and feed Beauty. But Emily envisioned that this time her mother would get out of the cart with her when they arrived. She would walk beside Emily to Beauty's stall without moaning about the flies or the mud. Emily and her mother would feed Beauty together, holding out apples and carrots on their open palms, stroking Beauty's shiny coat, laughing together. Emily's mother would make no exaggerated glances at her watch or sharp comments about having things to do. They would leave the stables only when the shadows were long and there was a nip in the air that suggested night was close.

Perhaps the most important aspect of Emily's imaginary scenario, and one that she might not have consciously created, was the presence of her mother's happiness. Emily was not used to seeing her mother genuinely happy and yet, in the imagined scenario, her mother was smiling and laughing. It wasn't her usual mocking laugh, or the overbearing, bordering-on-hysterical laugh that accompanied her drinking, but a soft, heartfelt laugh devoid of cynicism and pretence. Although Emily did not realise it, this, above all, was what she wished for: for her mother to be happy when she was with her.

Why did Emily think that this visit to the stables would be different from all the other visits? Why did she believe that this was the moment that her mother would discover true happiness? Was she picking up, on a subconscious level, the extra burden of her mother's guilt? Had she seen the stranger slipping from her mother's room in the morning or noticed her mother's increased absences? Perhaps she had, but it is unlikely that this was the sole reason Emily imagined that this specific visit would be different from those in the past. The reason Emily held such high hopes for this visit was that she had used up all her resources. She did not know if she had the ability to pretend any longer. Desperation had sown the seed of hope and watered it and nurtured it until it had grown into this one last impossible dream. Emily had thrown all that was left of her optimism, her belief, into this visit. Which is why it was so devastating for Emily when the afternoon turned out to be no different from any other on which they had gone to visit the horses.

It might have been less traumatic for Emily if her mother had forgotten about the visit completely; if Emily had been given a message, as sometimes happened, by her teacher that she was to get a lift home with Erica, who was in the other Grade One class and whose house was near Emily's. On the days that Erica's mother dropped her off, Emily knew that her mother would be home only much later in the evening. Emily would have been devastated, but she would have had reason to be angry with her mother. She would have felt justified in hating her. The disappointment would have been dramatic and final, reason to run away. But this, this half-hearted attempt at pretending to care, left Emily feeling far more hurt and betrayed than she would have had her mother simply been too self-absorbed to remember her promise. It left her with little justifiable reason for anger, because her mother had not actually broken her word.

Emily knew that it was not possible, but it was as though her mother had been able to see the scenario that she had so lovingly constructed in her mind and had wilfully destroyed it piece by piece. She had refused to stop at the shop on the way home from school, saying she didn't have the energy, and Emily had had to scrounge in the vegetable tray in the bottom of the fridge for food for Beauty. She had eventually found one rubbery carrot and two battered green apples. The base of one of the apples was covered in dark syrup that had leaked from a bottle somewhere higher up in the fridge and had slowly migrated down to the vegetable tray. Emily had washed the apples and the carrot, hoping that the cold water would freshen them up and make them look a little more edible, but they remained limp and bruised. Emily had put them into a bag and gone upstairs to get dressed. She had tried to convince herself that the rest of the afternoon could still go well, that things could change, but she had abandoned the thought completely and given in to despair when she was unable to find her riding boots. She had put on the jodhpurs and the shirt, but the outfit looked silly without the boots and so she had changed back into her school uniform. The collapse of each of the carefully created parts of her plan left her feeling dismayed and slightly disoriented.

Emily's mother had forgotten to charge the golf cart the previous evening and the battery was flat, so they had had to go to the stables in the car. Emily much preferred making the three-kilometre trip in the golf cart because she liked the feeling of the wind blowing in her face and the open space around her. There was also the bonus that the journey took longer in the golf cart.

They arrived at the stables, and before Emily got out of the car, her mother told her that she had ten minutes to do her thing with the horses before they had to leave. Ten minutes. Emily had spent an entire morning planning an outing that was to last ten minutes. Cherise never left the car, so she never saw the tears that streamed down Emily's cheeks as she fed her horse a rubbery carrot and two bruised apples.

Cherise went out to have coffee with a friend soon after she and Emily arrived back home from their outing to the stables. She did not notice her daughter's distress. On the contrary, she left the house shrouded in the glow of self-congratulation. Once Cherise had left, the housekeeper brought Emily, who had collapsed on the couch to watch a Barbie movie, a peanut butter sandwich, which Emily devoured hungrily. She had not eaten anything since the packet of chips she had had for lunch at school. The housekeeper also brought Emily her pair of riding boots, which she found beneath the stairs after Emily had left earlier that afternoon. The housekeeper had realised that Emily was upset, but she had attributed it to Emily having been unable to find her riding boots. She was surprised, therefore, when she handed Emily the boots and Emily threw them angrily across the room.

Emily had watched half of the Barbie movie when the thought occurred to her that she could go to the horses on her own. She and her brothers. She didn't need her mother in her dreams. She could still resurrect the afternoon. She picked up her riding boots and went to her room to get dressed. She took care with dressing, as though it was the first time that day that she was putting these specific clothes on. She buttoned closed each of the bow-buttons, making sure that they were correctly aligned. She pulled on the jodhpurs and the riding boots and then went to her mother's room to brush her hair. She scraped her hair back with her special-occasion pink, jewelled Alice band and looked at herself in the mirror on the wall of her mother's dressing room. Her next decision, to put on some make-up, was probably made more in belligerence than out of a real desire to wear make-up, because she used her mother's expensive Lancôme cosmetics instead of her own play make-up, something that she had been told numerous times she was not to do. She finished the look by liberally spraying herself with perfume from the figure-shaped bottle of eau de cologne on her mother's dressing table. It made her smell like her mother.

The housekeeper was watching a South African soapie on the small television set in her room and Cherise was still out at coffee, so no one saw Emily leave the house. She made her way down the hill, in the direction of the stables. It was fortunate that Emily lived in a security estate because had she not, she might well have fallen prey to a kidnapper desperate for ransom, or a sick-minded paedophile, or even an unscrupulous witchdoctor looking for pretty little girls' body parts. As it was, the only person she met on her journey down to the horses was Advocate Norman Ware, who was in the habit of taking a walk every evening along the same road on which Emily was travelling.

Emily was resting, sitting down on the wall of the bridge watching the catfish flop over each other in the shallow water below her, when Advocate Norman Ware walked past her. She was beginning to doubt her ability to follow through with her plan. She had never walked to the horses before and had not imagined that they would be so far away. She was also not entirely certain any more that the route to the stables was as simple as she remembered. Her brothers were of no help, because they had never been with her to visit the horses before. Her boots, worn only four times previously, were starting to hurt her feet, and the Alice band was pressing onto her head behind her ears and making it ache. Perhaps her distress was visible, because Advocate Norman Ware stopped as he walked past her and asked her if she was all right and where her mother was. His questions made Emily suddenly feel extremely tired – so tired that she felt that she could lie down on the bridge and immediately fall asleep. The disappointment of the afternoon, all of Emily's heartache and sorrow, welled up inside her and spilt down her cheeks. Advocate Norman Ware, who was not usually a particularly affectionate or demonstrative man, felt compelled to pick the little girl up and hug her. He cut his walk short and carried her back up the hill to her home. No one had noticed Emily's absence.

Chapter Six

THE OBJECT OF CHERISE Andreakos's misplaced affection was Dr Phillip Landers, a fellow resident in the San La Mer estate. Dr Phil, as he reassuringly encouraged his patients to call him, was the plastic surgeon whose services Cherise had engaged after Emily's birth, to ensure that she maintained the appearance of youth and beauty so desired by her husband. With time, her and Phil's arrangement had extended beyond the bounds of the operating theatre.

Phillip Landers had grown up in Cape Town, where he had attended one of the better-known private boys' schools. Initially he had not been accepted into the University of Cape Town's medical school, because he had not been a strong enough candidate academically, but his father, who was on numerous boards and held various influential positions, had paid multiple visits to the dean of the faculty of health sciences, and just prior to the start of the term in January, a place had been created for Phillip. The dream of Phillip becoming a doctor was shared equally between himself and his father. They both understood that the status conferred by money alone did not always carry enough weight in certain circles. A title, especially the title of doctor, implied a sense of honesty, integrity and stability that neither Phil nor his father had ever projected or would ever project independently.

Phil had managed to get through medical school by befriending the clever students and arse-licking the lecturers. His Machiavellian instincts, inherited from his father, were well tuned. Although he was never completely left out of any group work or social gathering, he was never popular at medical school. He was none of his peers' first, second or even third choice as clinical partner, and he usually received invitations to parties only by asking for them. It was an indictment of his life that at his very fancy twenty-first birthday celebration at the Table Bay Hotel, there were present more of his father's business associates (his father was, at the time, wooing select members of the Gambling Board) than Phil's friends. Those friends who did accept his invitation attended only for the gourmet meal and open bar. He earned the nickname 'Phil the till'. Sensitive, caring sorts might have taken pity on Phil had he not been so undeniably slimy.

After graduating from medical school, it did not take Phil long to realise that money could buy him the friends that he struggled so hard to make. It was probably this realisation that instigated Phil's decision to go into plastic surgery. Of course, there was also the knowledge that working as a cosmetic plastic surgeon would automatically bring him into contact with women of a certain age, appearance and disposition. Had Phil not specialised in cosmetic plastic surgery, there is no chance that he would have seen and felt as many breasts or as many vaginas as he did. In his defence, it must be noted that when he started specialising, he could not have known that vaginoplasties would become so popular, and thus he could never have predicted being exposed to so many wealthy vaginas.

Phillip Landers was also fully aware of the magical ability of money to transform the immediately obvious. If, for example, he arrived at a function in his Maserati, women failed to notice the acne scars that pitted his exceptionally oily skin. A similar principle applied to his credit cards. If he flashed his platinum private-bank cards around, his lack of orthodontic treatment became far less obvious. Designer suits hid his paunch and spindly legs; expensive fragrances disguised his halitosis. Although Phil Landers was undeniably questionable, the fact that so many women fell for him within the circles in which he moved was a far greater indictment of them than of him.

Phillip had initially opened a practice in Cape Town, which made sense because that was where all his contacts were. He called his practice 'Re!nvent Yourself' and employed beauty therapists to perform chemical peels and manage the laser hair and wrinkle removal, while he personally offered Botox injections, fillers and, of course, plastic surgery. After only two years, however, he had been forced to move, with rather more haste than he liked, to Durban. The reason for his hurried transfer was that one of his ex-patients decided to bring a case of sexual harassment against him. Unfortunately, she was very public with her accusations and Phillip's fledgling practice nosedived. He learnt his lesson: he made sure that in future he chose more wisely the women with whom he intended to have affairs. Re!nvent Yourself opened in the wealthy, body-conscious suburb of Umhlanga Rocks, and Phillip took up residence in the nearby San La Mer estate. Had Dr Phillip Landers not been so pretentious and materialistic, and had he chosen to live in humbler surroundings, he would never have ended up playing the role that he did in Advocate Norman Ware's murder.

Philip Landers lived in the new section of the estate, which was where most of the nouveau riche lived. The estate was divided, by very obscure and ill-defined geographical and legislative barriers, into an old section and a new section. The two sections were not even distinguished chronologically, so there was no logical reason for them to be labelled 'old' and 'new'. It might have been that the denomination was a reflection of the nature of the respective residents more than anything else. Generally, the houses in the old section tended to be colonial in style, with big sash windows and enough dark wood in their interiors to have obliterated an entire teak plantation. They were stately and reminiscent of the 'good old days'. The owners of houses in the old section tended to prefer ceiling fans to air-conditioning units, which they felt made them sick; they used inverted commas a lot; and they always had rooms next to the garage in which their 'domestics' could sleep. The houses in the new section were largely ostentatious and gaudy with excessive pillars and far too much glass to be practical. They all had obligatory jacuzzis. By far the most ostentatious, pillared and jacuzzied of these houses belonged to Phillip Landers.

—·—

Although Dr Phil was having an affair with Cherise Andreakos, he was by no means having an affair exclusively with her. He was simultaneously shagging his attractive young receptionist; a middle-aged advocate on whom he had recently done a complete makeover, consisting of breast augmentation, abdominoplasty, liposuction, rhytidectomy and vaginoplasty, and who now looked twenty-five; and a twenty-year-old who was saving up for the breast augmentation that she believed would accelerate her modelling career to the illustrious domain of international cover pages. With the help of the occasional Viagra tablet (fondly referred to as the 'blue diamond' by Dr Phil), he was able to meet the physical expectations of his demanding schedule; mentally, however, he fell short. His mistake was not one of shoddy planning. He did not mix up a liaison or substitute one lover's name with another. He made certain that his partners' social circles did not overlap and that none of them shared the same hairdresser, beauty therapist or personal trainer. His mistake was not an oversight or a coincidence; it was the result of pride.

It tickled Phil's ego to book the appointments of his current lovers consecutively, and so he booked Cherise before the middle-aged makeover, whom he booked before the aspiring model. It boosted his manhood disproportionately to walk into his waiting room and see the three women (and, of course, his receptionist) he was screwing, all sitting next to each other oblivious of their common link. He had not accounted for the intuition and intelligence of his middle-aged makeover, however, perhaps because she now looked so young and naive. He would pay dearly for this oversight.

Many people have the incorrect impression, frequently perpetuated by books and movies, that ghosts like the dark. They fear ghosts, and look out for them in cemeteries and abandoned houses with creaky doors. They switch on lights and seek the company of others in order to avoid ghosts. In fact, spirits like the light. They are attracted to people in a similar but less fatal way to that in which moths are attracted to a candle flame: with an inevitability and an unconscious magnetism. Ghosts like company; they like to listen in on conversations and to pretend that they too can contribute. They ache for some kind of connection with another. Perhaps it is a confirmation of their existence for which they are continually searching. Eight-year-old Clarissa Mallory knew all of this because she could see spirits as clearly as she could see everyone else around her.

It was for this reason that when, on the third of November, Clarissa saw Advocate Norman Ware walking past her house as he usually did in the late afternoon, she was not entirely sure whether he was dead or alive. It was only when she examined him more closely and noticed, among other things, his missing fingers, ears and nose that she realised he must have moved on into the afterlife. Clarissa had observed that the recently dead often have an expression of bewilderment on their faces, as though they were struggling to figure out the terms of their new existence. Although it was difficult to judge the specific expression on Advocate Norman Ware's face because it had been so disfigured, she imagined that he would be feeling lost and overwhelmed. She raised her hand and waved at him and saw a tiny flicker of hope in his dull eyes. He manoeuvred his lipless mouth into a smile and briefly raised a palm and five stumps at her. Clarissa was not disgusted – she had seen far worse. On the contrary, the gesture made her happy. It pleased her to be reminded that she had a function and that, despite her external appearance, there were those who were happy to see her.

Clarissa had known from birth, with the same certainty

with which she knew what had happened in the past and what would happen in the future, that she was different from the people around her. Some people would label her a psychic, but Clarissa had none of the psychic's usual desire to change or make known the course of destiny. She understood that she had a different job to do. Her function was to comfort those spirits who had left the physical world and moved on to the metaphysical. She was a link, a bridge, between the two worlds. She knew that ghosts were those spirits who, for some reason or other, were not yet ready to forgo their physical form, and she was there to help them confirm the existence of their soul while they learnt to accept and let go. It was immaterial that she was unable to speak, because her role was with the dead, not with the living.

Clarissa realised that she had been born where she had because there were many spirits on the San La Mer estate who needed her help. In a few years' time, after her mother's death, she would be moved to an institution for disabled children and there would be many there who would need her help too. But for now she existed to comfort those around her.

There were a number of Zulu ghosts on the estate: five strong young men dressed in fighting gear and carrying long metal spears in their hands, all of them riddled with bullet holes; a young woman, naked except for a torn, bloodied leather *kaross*; two slightly older women with the swollen bellies of pregnancy; and an ancient man, wrinkled like a piece of leather. It was odd to see an older ghost. Older people had often made peace with the mortality of their physical body and so seldom had difficulty leaving it behind. It was younger people, people who had met an untimely death and who had too many ties to the living, that found it difficult to leave.

There was the spirit of a young white man, a cyclist who had been knocked over by a car on the highway that ran adjacent to the San La Mer estate. There was a lady in her mid-forties who walked the estate wearing a pink-and-purple paper crown. She had killed herself on Christmas day by drinking rat poison, while her husband and two young daughters were playing in the garden outside. When she saw the crowned lady, Clarissa often found herself sobbing at the immensity of the suffering the woman must have endured to do what she did. There was a builder who had died during the construction of one of the San La Mer mansions, after scaffolding had fallen on him. And, of course, there were the twelve teenage girls with hacked-off breasts.

Clarissa was saddened by the fact that the ghosts were unable to see one another and interact among themselves in the way that living people were. She imagined that it would be a big comfort to them if they could share stories and cry together, if they could reach some sort of closure by expressing their fears and worries and regrets. Since they did not really exist, however, except on the strength of their own belief, that was impossible, and the only contact or feedback they ever received was from Clarissa.

Had Clarissa been aware of the prejudices and snobbery of certain San La Mer residents, the fact that the estate was so densely and diversely populated without their knowledge might have amused her. But although she could see the metaphysical very clearly, Clarissa lacked insight into the peculiarities of human nature and the intricacies of social structure, and thus she was oblivious of the sense of exclusivity adopted by the residents of San La Mer.

Chapter Seven

A NUMBER OF QUESTIONS about the murder of Advocate Norman Ware plagued the police detectives assigned to investigating the case. Many of these questions revolved around the murder weapon, or weapons. Why, for example, had the murderer so carefully concealed the instrument that the investigators believed had been used to torture Advocate Norman Ware and yet so callously discarded the actual murder weapon? Was there further evidence of the torture instrument that the criminal wished to hide? Or were they dealing with a set-up? These questions would linger until the very end of the investigation, and none of the detectives would be entirely certain, once the case had been tied up, that they had been adequately answered.

The murder weapon itself, the object used to kill Advocate Norman Ware, was found hidden in a plumbago bush close to the murder scene. Even though it was an unusual choice for a murder weapon, there was no doubt that it had played a key role in the death of the victim. The side of Advocate Norman Ware's head, just above his temple, contained an imprint of the cherub's face. It was highly likely to have been as a result of this blunt trauma to the head that Advocate Norman Ware had eventually died. Although the mutilation that he had suffered – the careful, almost surgical removal of his ears, lips, nose, fingers, toes, penis and scrotum – was horrific, even the initial investigators at the scene realised that it alone would have been unlikely to have resulted in his death. The investigators' immediate impression was that Advocate Norman Ware had been tortured, possibly in an attempt to get sensitive or important information out of him, and then killed. Again, there was the vaguely disturbing incongruity that whoever had tortured the victim had apparently done so as a professional, and yet the choice of murder weapon and the sloppy manner in which it was discarded were highly suggestive of an amateur at work.

The murder weapon was a bronze statuette of a cherub. One of the investigators described it to the press as a weapon of chance and not of choice. He could not imagine that any professional or seasoned killer would choose to use a statue of a chubby winged baby as a murder weapon. There was something of the ridiculous to it. This statement to the media by the garrulous police officer was hasty and careless: although the weapon appeared to be one of chance, which would imply that the murder had not been premeditated, the apparent torture suggested otherwise. The only possible explanation for the incongruity presented by the choice of murder weapon and the obviously premeditated mutilation was that the bronze cherub held specific meaning both for the deceased and for the killer.

The fatal bronze Cupid's emissary appeared at first glance to be kitsch and garish, but it was actually an expensive artwork that had been crafted in Italy by a prominent and well-known sculptor. There is the possibility that in Tuscany, among overgrown trellised vines and ancient cracked marble fountains, the statuette would have looked beguiling and would have denoted a sense of place, but in San La Mer, among the Bali-inspired pillars and the jacuzzis, it looked distinctly distasteful.

The bronze cherub was forty-three centimetres tall and weighed just over four kilograms. It was standing on the tips of its toes with its wings spread, as though poised to lift off its metal base and fly up into the heavens. Its visage – the chubby cheeks and heart-shaped mouth and wide eyes – was slightly obscured by traces of Advocate Norman Ware's blood, to which had adhered loose dirt and a few pieces of grass. The curvaceous body of the cherub was inelegantly splattered with the vomit of the groundsman who had found the body. Jackson had not realised, when he ran from the men's bathroom in which he had found the victim and disgorged the contents of his stomach onto the bushes he was supposed to be trimming, that he would be obscuring very good evidence. When Detective De Villiers, hands clad in soft cotton gloves, gingerly removed the cherub from the odorous bush, he had hoped that he would be able to lift fingerprints from the statuette. That would have presented him with a unique situation: a murder weapon; fingerprints on the murder weapon; and a limited pool of suspects (on account of the security on the estate, there were records of everyone who had been in the estate on the night of the murder) from whom to take comparative fingerprints. Unfortunately, his job was not to be so easy. The vomit splatters had almost completely obscured the fingerprints, rendering them useless. It was a strange twist of fate that had Jackson not vomited on the bronze cherub, the outcome of the murder investigation would have been very different.

———◆———

It would be easy to excuse Titus Mokotla's avarice, questionable morals and selfishness as the result of a haphazard and dysfunctional upbringing, except that there are many people who have had as disjointed a youth and have not become greedy, self-serving tycoons. Whether it was the cause of Titus's faults or not, there was no denying that he had had a difficult youth. Titus had been brought up largely by his grandmother. His mother, who was severely mentally disabled, had been raped by her uncle, and the consequence of this was Titus's conception. Because the uncle, a gardener, was the sole breadwinner in a household of five adults and eighteen children, he had never been kicked out or called to account for his behaviour, and thus Titus had two younger sisters and a younger brother. Two of his siblings were severely mentally handicapped – the result of an ill-defined genetic syndrome. They presented not only a huge financial drain on the household, but also took up most of the time and energy of Titus's grandmother. This left Titus with little adult supervision or care, especially since his father showed no interest in his children's upbringing.

Titus had attended school erratically. This was not entirely his fault, but was also the result of a teacher who seldom came to work sober and an education system that allowed for forty-five children in one class. The consequence of this was that there was no stability in Titus's life and he had had no strong male models on which to mould himself. It was probably for this reason more than any political persuasion that he aligned himself so strongly with the ANC Youth League.

Titus was first exposed to the ANC shortly after its unbanning, in 1991, when he was enthusiastically drafted into the children's social wing, the Masupatsela. There he found structure, solidarity and numerous older males onto whom he could transfer the role of the father figure that he so craved. It may have been that initially Titus was idealistic and hopeful; that he was caught up in the wave of optimism and hope that swept across South Africa in the early 1990s. And perhaps there was a time when he believed in equality for all, and in the fair redistribution of wealth and power, but by the time of Advocate Norman Ware's murder, those beliefs had long since left him. Titus had taken full advantage of his ANC credentials to be awarded tender after tender and had made his fortune in this way. Thus, in November 2011, he was an extremely wealthy member of the upper echelons of the ANC, with numerous luxurious residences, including one in the San La Mer estate, over twenty exclusive cars and many other symbols of wealth. Titus lacked the insight to see the irony of his position.

With his increasing wealth, Titus Mokotla had developed an odd obsession with the American Mafia, mostly based on what he had seen in movies and on television. Perhaps it was the Mafia's connection with corruption, bribery, money laundering and power, in many ways so similar to his, which formed the bond of attraction. Or, since Titus was a suave and snappy dresser, it might have been the glamorous appearance of the Mafiosi with whom Titus identified. Of course, there is also the possibility that Titus was attracted to the Mafia's strict code of hierarchy and structure, something that the ANC was rapidly losing and that had initially drawn Titus to the bosom of the political party. Whatever it was, by the time of Advocate Norman Ware's death Titus had modelled himself on the American Mafia kings. He was an active member of Rick Porello's website – AmericanMafia.com – and spent hours on chat forums with other Mafia enthusiasts or buying American Mafia memorabilia, with which he decorated his numerous opulent residences. He liked to dress in what he thought was Mafia style, and so he always wore suits, either black wool or white linen, which he had specially made by an Indian tailor in Durban, and shiny leather brogues. When out and about, he would often wear a traditional Mafia-style fedora.

Titus Mokotla was wearing one of these Mafia-style centre-dent fedoras on the afternoon of Wednesday the second of November, the day before Advocate Norman Ware's murder. He was sitting at the pool area of the San La Mer estate, in which, it has been mentioned, he owned a palatial mansion, enjoying a cocktail while bestowing equal admiration on the view of the pools and on Estelle, the waitress who was serving him. Titus had noticed Estelle before and found her to be extremely pleasing on the eye. He liked the way the blouse of her blue uniform gaped temptingly at the buttons, revealing just a hint of black brassière, and he approved of her well-rounded calves and narrow ankles. He planned on taking her home with him later that afternoon once she had finished her shift, and to that end was obviously, and rather lewdly, flirting with her while she served him. It was not the fact that Titus was married that would eventually preclude Estelle's going home with him, but the fact that he was so intoxicated that he would cut his finger, allowing Estelle the opportunity to make a hasty escape.

By five o'clock, half an hour before the restaurant was due to close, Titus was drunk enough to believe that he was irresistible to Estelle. He decided to have one more drink and a last cigar before suggesting to the object of his admiration that she accompany him home. Titus ordered himself a double Johnnie Walker Blue on the rocks and removed a Romeo y Julieta cigar from his pocket cigar case. It was while he was clipping the end of his cigar that his plans to take Estelle home were foiled. He sliced open the top of his finger. Although the cut was superficial, not nearly deep enough to need stitches, it bled profusely. Embarrassed at his clumsiness and at the evidence of his intoxicated state, Titus quickly hid the injured finger beneath the table so that Estelle would not notice it. As soon as she had her back to him, he hurried to the men's bathroom to rinse the cut and contain the bleeding. Estelle had not seen his accident with the cigar clippers, but she had observed him making his way to the bathroom and recognised it as her chance to escape. She hastily cashed up and ran to catch the five o'clock shuttle. It would lift her to the estate gates and from there she would take a taxi home. When Titus emerged from the bathroom, finger swaddled in toilet paper, he found that he was being offered the bill by the male restaurant manager. Sore and disgruntled, Titus nevertheless sat down determined not to let the adverse intervention of fate ruin his evening. He bought the remainder of the bottle of Johnnie Walker Blue from the restaurant manager, who was all too happy to sell it to Titus for an exorbitant price, and made himself comfortable on his deck chair. He sat drinking, watching the sky darken, while the last of the restaurant staff cleaned tables and then made their way to the shuttle collection point. By six o'clock, Titus was alone at the pool area.

It would have been nice to say that Titus spent the early evening in a lonely, drunken nostalgia, reminiscing over times when he was more idealistic and when life was worth more to him than sex, power and money; that he made resolutions to become a better person and to spend the rest of his days in philanthropic generosity. Unfortunately, this was not the case. Instead, Titus thought about an appointment that he had the following day with a representative of the minister of environmental affairs, to whom he would have to pay an exorbitant sum of money to ensure that the endangered mistbelt moss frog did not threaten his plans for a large pine plantation, and about his sister, who had approached him for money to pay for her child's schooling. By the time Titus Mokotla had finished the bottle of whisky, it was dark. He stumbled from the deck chair to his golf cart, which was parked in the pool area parking lot in one of the bays designated for golf carts. Titus drove out of the parking lot at twenty-five minutes to eight. He managed, through luck rather than skill, not to crash his golf cart on the kilometre-long drive home. When he reached his home, he made his way unsteadily up to his bedroom and collapsed into bed. He would regain consciousness the following morning, at half past seven.

—•—

Noluthando Gwala felt no guilt about the job that she did, for she saw it simply for what it was, as a means of earning enough money to support the two children and seven grandchildren who depended on her. Her life had not been easy since her husband had deserted her for a younger, more beautiful woman, and if fate had thrown this one bone at her, she was not about to throw it back. Of course, she was not talking about her cleaning job, about which her feelings were ambivalent – although if it had not been for the domestic worker position, she would never have stumbled across her other, more lucrative source of income.

Noluthando had been working for Shine Cleaning Services for three years. When she started the job, she had been living in a one-roomed shack with two of her children, both grown up and both unemployed, and seven of her grandchildren, who ranged in age between two and eight years. Three of these children were orphans: their mother, who was Noluthando's third daughter, had recently died of AIDS, leaving her children in the care of their grandmother. The wage of eighty rands a day that Noluthando was paid by Shine Cleaning Services barely covered the cost of the rent and of food for her family, but Noluthando was acutely aware that it was better than nothing. It was for this reason that Noluthando made sure that she worked harder than the other cleaning ladies at Shine Cleaning Services, that she was always on time, and that even when she was sick with fever or plagued by her arthritis, she went to work. She could not afford to lose her job. Over time, she came to be regarded by her managers as one of their more dependable employees.

Shine Cleaning Services was licensed to provide domestic workers to the residents of the San La Mer estate. It was a small, family-run company, whose owners liked to believe that they treated their employees well. They were proud of the fact that they gave their ladies uniforms instead of making them pay for them, and that they made monthly contributions on their behalf to the Unemployment Insurance Fund. They would also readily point out that they gave their employees paid sick leave and holiday leave, which was far more than most other equivalent companies offered. Residents of San La Mer could use the services of Shine on either a regular or an ad hoc basis. It was while Noluthando was on one of these longer-term contracts that she stumbled across a means of making far more money than she was earning from Shine.

The family for which Noluthando was to clean on a regular basis had recently moved to San La Mer from Johannesburg, after having been hijacked for the fourth time. They explained to the receptionist at Shine Cleaning Services that they had been unable to bring their previous domestic worker with them because she had a family of her own in Johannesburg, and so they would require the services of a housekeeper during the week. They stipulated that they wanted someone trustworthy, because they were away a lot, and someone unobtrusive, because they did not want to notice anyone in the house when they were not away. Noluthando seemed like the perfect person for the job.

The house that Noluthando was to clean was in an obscure cul-de-sac in a forested area of San La Mer. Noluthando had been dropped off at the top of the short road with the instruction to call her supervisor to pick her up when she was finished for the day. She walked down the cul-de-sac, which was on a hill, and made her way to Number 3 Malachite Close. There were only four houses in the road. Noluthando passed the entrances to two of them on her way to her new place of employment. Both houses were quiet and closed up: holiday houses aired only a few times a year. The house that Noluthando was to work in was a double-storey Tuscan-style villa that backed onto a green belt of preserved coastal forest. Steps led down to the entrance. On one side of the stairway, a fountain bubbled pleasantly. A cement Venus, emerging from her moss-covered clamshell, smiled at Noluthando as she made her way to the front door and knocked on the brass knocker.

The woman who opened the door for Noluthando was in her early forties. She seemed pleasant, although rather distracted. It was as though she was unable to focus her attention on one person or thing for longer than a few seconds. Her eyes darted from place to place incessantly. She introduced herself to Noluthando, either as Josie or Rosie (Noluthando was unable to hear which and so subsequently only ever called her Ma'am), and gave her a cursory tour of the house. The introductory tour ended at an outside bathroom, which the woman indicated was for Noluthando's use. By the time Noluthando had changed into her uniform and found her way back to the kitchen, the woman had left for the day. Noluthando washed the breakfast dishes and then moved on to the bedrooms. From what she could ascertain from the unmade beds, the interior decor of the bedrooms and the photographs on the wall, the family comprised four members: mother, father, daughter and son. Noluthando supposed that the children were younger than ten but old enough to be going to school already. The boy appeared to be obsessed with sport of all kinds, while the girl's room was decorated with posters of *High School Musical*. The floors of both bedrooms were scattered with toys.

Perhaps because she had been working at San La Mer for a number of years and had become used to excess, the opulence of the household did not surprise Noluthando. It did not enter her mind to wonder at the fact that each child had their own bathroom attached to their bedroom; to condemn the fact that the house was so large that four of the rooms appeared to be unused on a daily basis; or to compare the contents of the toy boxes with the measly few toys owned by her own grandchildren. Noluthando appeared to notice none of this. Instead, she noticed the cobwebs behind the bedside tables and the fingerprints on the windows, and focused on these.

By lunchtime, Noluthando, who was naturally a garrulous person, had begun to feel lonely. One might imagine that after the hustle and bustle of her own house, after the noise of seven children and three adults packed into a single thin-walled room, Noluthando would appreciate a few hours of quiet and solitude, but this was not the case. The silence made her edgy. It echoed around the large house and made normal noises louder than they should be. Somehow, the stillness seemed to drag time out. It was for this reason that Noluthando decided to take a walk over her lunch break and see if there was anyone with whom she could talk. It was this decision, this decision to go for a short walk to seek out company, that would impact irrevocably not only on Noluthando's life but, later, on the outcome of the investigation into Advocate Norman Ware's murder.

Noluthando remembered that the first two houses in the cul-de-sac had appeared to be unoccupied, but she knew that there was a fourth and hoped that there might be a domestic worker there whom she could befriend. She walked the few hundred metres down the road to the entrance of the fourth house, hoping that she would be able to see from the road whether the house was occupied or not. Unfortunately, although the garage was close to the road, the house seemed to be deeper in the forest. Access was down a narrow footpath. Noluthando hesitated for a few minutes, and then began to make her way gingerly down the footpath. The branches of the trees on either side had encroached onto the path, as though they were unhappy with the intrusion into their territory, and scratched Noluthando's arms as she walked. Fallen sticks and twigs cracked disconcertingly beneath her feet, and somewhere in a bush a robin trilled. The density of the vegetation meant that the light was poor and Noluthando had to concentrate on where she was walking in order not to fall. It was because of this, because she was looking down at where she was placing her feet, that she noticed the finger. It was poking up from the ground, as though it was a new shoot. Except that new shoots don't generally have painted nails. Noluthando felt a coldness crawl up her spine. No good could come of a finger poking up from the ground like that, berating God. Noluthando turned around and went back the way she had come. She was sure that there was no one in that dwelling whom she wanted to befriend.

—•—

If Noluthando was a little distracted during the first few days of her new cleaning assignment, she could hardly be blamed for it. It was not usual to see digits growing from the ground, and Noluthando could not stop her mind from thinking about that finger, with its pale pink painted nail, which she had seen sticking up from the loamy soil of the forest floor. The garage to the house-with-the-finger opened onto the road and was visible from the kitchen window of the house that Noluthando cleaned. She stared at the garage while she washed up, wondering what dark secrets it held. After observing for a few days, she learnt that the owner of the house left home every morning at ten minutes to eight and returned at ten minutes past five in the evening. There was no variation to his routine. He didn't look like the type of person whom Noluthando would imagine to have a finger poking up in his garden: he had no heavy gold chains or tattoos; no bulging biceps beneath muscle shirts; no slick black glasses and crocodile-skin shoes. On the contrary, his appearance was extremely conservative, bordering on banal. He looked about thirty-five, with dark hair that he wore short and in a side parting. His skin was pale and Noluthando thought that he must have a job that kept him indoors most of the time. He was tall but thin, effeminate even. So normal was his appearance and behaviour that Noluthando began to wonder whether he was even aware of the digit protruding from his garden path.

Over the next few weeks, instead of fading, the memory of the finger began to haunt Noluthando. She saw it everywhere: on the washing line as she was hanging up the washing; in the bottom of her coffee cup, stuck in the sugar that her stirring had not dissolved; in the bed beside her grandchildren when she put them to sleep. Eventually she decided that there was nothing she could do to rid her mind of the finger but to revisit it.

One morning Noluthando waited until she had seen the man leave and then made her way to the neighbouring house. She walked slowly down the path with her heart beating in her throat. She looked down as she walked to be sure that she would not miss the finger, but she saw nothing other than rotting leaves and snapped twigs and the odd tawny mushroom. The digit appeared to have gone. She felt her heart lighten a little; perhaps she had imagined it. Perhaps it had not been a finger after all. Noluthando continued along the path as though driven by a will other than her own. She knew that she shouldn't, that she had no business to, but she needed to clear her mind of the possibility that the finger had ever existed and the only way to do that was to see this journey through to its completion. She had thought of an excuse should someone catch her. She was coming to borrow some sugar; madam had run out and she needed sugar in her coffee. Isn't that what neighbours did, lend and borrow sugar? Her biggest concern was being caught trespassing and losing her job as a result. She never considered the possibility that the next finger poking up from the ground might be hers.

———◦———

The house appeared to be empty. All of the curtains were drawn except for those on the kitchen window, so Noluthando was unable to see much of the inside of the dwelling. She knocked twice on the door, but no one answered. Nothing seemed at all out of the ordinary. Noluthando chuckled at her overactive imagination and turned around to make her way back down the path through the forest, convinced that the finger had been nothing but an apparition that she could now put to rest. It was instinct, not training in the methods of detection, that made Noluthando stop a quarter of the way back along the path. At first she didn't even know why she had stopped. It was only after her conscious mind had had time to catch up with her subconscious that she realised that it was because the ground a metre from the path had recently been disturbed. The sticks and fallen leaves that formed the ground cover everywhere else had been covered with loose soil. She walked gingerly towards the turned earth and dislodged a chunk with her foot. The soil came away easily. A few more kicks at the ground revealed a slender, pale foot with prettily painted toenails. Noluthando thought that it must be witchcraft that had preserved the foot so perfectly and had stopped it from stinking. (In fact, it was formalin, but there was no way that she could know that.) Noluthando removed a little more of the soil and the lower leg was revealed. She presumed, from the proportions of the area of disturbed soil, that the leg had not been buried in isolation, and that there was probably another leg as well as a torso, arms and head beneath the loamy ground. She had no desire to confirm her suspicions. Noluthando fled the burial site and ran to the relative safety of her outside bathroom, where she sat on the toilet and tried to catch her breath and gather her thoughts. By the end of the day, Noluthando had decided that it would be best for her to simply forget that she had ever seen the buried foot. There were a couple of reasons for this, not least among them the fact that she had had no reason to be walking along the path. Whatever was going on in the neighbouring house had nothing to do with her, and interfering would be likely only to bring about trouble and jeopardise her job.

The decision to pretend that the foot did not exist was one with which Noluthando felt at peace, and she would probably have left the foot, and the body that she presumed was still attached to it, well alone had it not been for three random events that happened to occur on the same day, just under a month later.

The first was that her granddaughter gave her a letter from their landlord. She handed it to Noluthando as Noluthando was about to leave for work. For some reason, perhaps because the envelope looked very official and had a red sticker on the front, Noluthando did not leave it at home to open in the afternoon but took it with her. She opened it at the taxi rank, while she was waiting in the queue for a taxi. The letter informed her that from the following month her rent would be going up. It would no longer be R250 a month but would now be R450 a month. The first instalment of the new, higher rent would be due on the first of the month, which happened to be in five days' time, the following Monday. The letter filled Noluthando with more worry than the foot had. Unless she won the Lotto – which was unlikely, as she had diligently entered weekly for the past nine years and had not yet been rewarded with more than thirty rands – she could not afford the extra rent. She had already asked for an advance on her salary because she had had to buy new school shoes for two of her grandchildren. She owed money to her neighbour, money that she had borrowed to buy groceries, and she owed R700 on her Edgars account, which she had been trying to pay off for the past eight months. Noluthando got into the taxi and stared out of the window as the vehicle made its way through the township and then onto the highway that led to the wealthier suburbs. She would have to move her family, but she didn't know if she would be able to find a cheaper place to stay – certainly not in five days.

The second event that took place on that day was that the man-with-the-finger changed his routine. Noluthando almost missed it because she had been thinking about exactly how she was going to ask the lady whose house she cleaned if she could borrow some money, and so she had not been paying attention, as she usually did, to the happenings at the house next door. She only became aware that there was something unusual going on because, while she was outside hanging up the washing, she heard a strange noise coming from the neighbouring driveway. Noluthando hurried inside to look out of the kitchen window so she could get a better view of what was happening. Not only was the man-with-the-finger emerging from his home later than normal, but he was wearing shorts and a T-shirt instead of his usual suit, and he was pulling a large suitcase behind him. It was the wheels of the suitcase that made the noise that had alerted Noluthando. He put the suitcase into the back of his car and drove off. Noluthando could only presume that he was going on a holiday.

Noluthando plucked up the courage later in the day to ask the lady for whom she cleaned to lend her some money. She explained the situation and promised that she would pay her back as soon as she got paid. Noluthando realised, before she had even finished talking, that the lady was going to refuse. She had shut her eyes off, as though she had closed them without lowering the lids. 'This is exactly why I employed a cleaning company,' she had said, 'so that I don't have to deal with issues like this. I can't afford to get emotionally involved with my staff. I'm sorry, but no.'

The third thing that happened to Noluthando that day took place while she was on her way home. She was sitting in the front of the taxi, and when it stopped at a red traffic light, a man shoved a wad of printed pieces of paper through the window at her. The taxi pulled off and Noluthando reached back and handed the pamphlets out. They were advertising the services of 'Mama Doctor', who promised to cure all sorts of things. Noluthando glanced at the list to see if there was anything unusual on it. She saw advertisements such as these often and they always claimed to cure the same ills. It was while Noluthando was idly reading through the list of maladies for which the sangoma promised a cure that her great idea came to her. There was no flashing of a light bulb above her head or jumping up and shouting eureka. It was as though the idea had existed within her forever and she had only to uncover it. She smiled to herself as she folded one of the pamphlets and placed it safely in her bag. And for the briefest of moments, as the weight of her worries lifted temporarily, she looked beautiful again, as she had before her pretty daughter had stolen her beauty.

——•——

The following day, after checking that the garage of the man-with-the-finger was still empty, Noluthando walked down the garden path. She had in her hand a gardening spade and a pair of pruning shears that she had found in a box underneath the stairs of the house that she cleaned. The shears were heavy-duty, their function to trim small branches rather than just leaves, and the blades were sharp. Even so, Noluthando was surprised at how little mess there was in the end; at how cleanly, almost, the toes had come off. She had expected lots of blood (she had even brought a cloth with her, in order to wipe off the pruning shears after completing her job and to clean up any other blood that might have spilt), but her assumptions were based on what she had seen on television programmes. She had never before had personal experience in amputating digits from a corpse. She sealed the toes in a ziplock bag that she had brought with her and placed the plastic bag in her handbag. When she went past security on her way out of the estate that afternoon, she hid the ziplock bag in her bra. She didn't want to risk the security guards finding the toes in her handbag when they did their routine afternoon search of it. Instead of getting on her usual taxi, Noluthando found one that was headed for Stanger. She had warned her daughter that morning that she would be home a little later than usual.

Throughout the drive to Stanger, the toes burned Noluthando's breast where they lay hidden. It was as though she had taken a piece of coal from the fire and stuffed it, while it was still glowing, into her bosom. She imagined that soon the toes would burn through the cotton of her dress and her fellow commuters on the taxi would see her shame. Noluthando reassured herself that she was doing nothing wrong. The woman whose toes she had stolen had been dead anyway. It wasn't as though she, Noluthando, had killed the lady. She had merely removed the toes from her dead body. And if she didn't do this, if this plan didn't work out, she and her children and her grandchildren would have no roof over their heads by Monday.

Mama Doctor's room was above a wholesaler. Noluthando had to climb up a narrow staircase that stank of cat pee and rotting vegetables to reach the door. She had rung the bell and Mama Doctor had answered almost immediately, ushering Noluthando into the darkened room. Noluthando could not help noticing the disfiguring purple stain that covered half of Mama Doctor's cheek. It made her shiver, made her acutely aware of what exactly it was that she was dealing with. Mama Doctor leant over Noluthando and sniffed at the air around her, as though smelling out Noluthando's business with her. Noluthando recoiled slightly. The woman scared her. Eager to be gone as quickly as possible, Noluthando reached into her bra and retrieved the toes. They were pale and bloodless and looked almost like strange fruits in the ziplock bag. Mama Doctor took the bag and studied the toes. For the briefest of moments, Noluthando thought she saw a look of revulsion on the woman's face, but she hid it so quickly that Noluthando could not be sure it had been real or whether her imagination had been playing tricks on her. Mama Doctor took four hundred rands from a leather purse that hung around her neck and handed it to Noluthando. Her expression was stony and Noluthando knew that it would be useless to try to bargain with the woman. Besides, Noluthando was more than happy with the money. She was struggling to contain her delight; to keep her expression neutral. She had had no idea that body parts were worth so much. The four hundred rands was the easiest money Noluthando had ever earned. It meant that she would be able to stay in her house for the next month; that her grandchildren would have a home; that there would be a little extra food on the table this week. Any hesitation Noluthando had felt before, any guilt or moral vacillation, disappeared with the feel of the crumpled blue notes in her hand.

Through observing and snooping, certain patterns became apparent to Noluthando over the next two years. She learnt that the man-with-the-finger went away once every three months, for two weeks at a time. Ten days after his return, there would be a new grave. She figured out that the big suitcase was not only for clothes, but to transport the bodies home in. She didn't know what he did with the bodies between the time he came home from his holiday and when he buried them. She tried not to think about it too much.

Noluthando never opened the whole grave: she had no desire to see the faces of the man's victims. She simply dug up limbs and exposed appendages, which she systematically cut off and sold to Mama Doctor.

Initially, Noluthando told herself that she would tell someone, the police or the estate security, about the buried corpses. She convinced herself that as soon as she had paid off her Edgars account, or purchased her own home, or bought school clothes for her grandchildren, or paid for her daughter's funeral, she would let the police know about the man. She could deny any involvement; no one would ever know that it was she who had been desecrating the bodies. But the money was too good, and after a year of selling body parts to Mama Doctor, Noluthando accepted the fact that she did not have the strength of character to give up what fate had so generously thrown her way.

Chapter Eight

ANGELA MALLORY COUNTED her blessings each night as she lay in bed trying to fall asleep. She did this to convince herself that there was a God, and that she had not been completely forsaken. She thanked the God whose existence she doubted for her husband, who loved her and who had endless patience, and she thanked Him for her son, who was a strong, healthy boy, and she thanked Him for the beautiful house in which her family lived and for the fact that they didn't have to lock their doors at night, and she thanked Him that she had good friends who brought her meals or flowers or home-baked cakes, and she thanked Him that she had some of the best doctors in the country looking after her. She found it difficult, on certain days, to thank God for her daughter. That didn't mean that she loved her daughter any less than she loved her husband or her son.

The reason Angela was struggling with the concept of an all-loving, all-forgiving God was that she was thirty-three, with two young children, and was dying of cervical cancer. It would have been easier for Angela if she had had something to blame the cancer on – if she had been infected with human papillomavirus, or if she had forgotten to go for her yearly Papanicolaou smears, or if there had been a family history of cancer, or if she had been a smoker – but she did not have a single risk factor on which to pin the blame for her diagnosis, so it fell by default onto God.

Angela had tested negative for the strains of human papillomavirus that were linked to cervical cancer. Angela ate healthily, exercised at least five times a week, didn't smoke and drank only socially. Angela had never skipped a check-up and had never had an abnormal smear. That was why it seemed so terribly unfair to her that her cells had, without any recognisable trigger, mutated to become cancerous, and had then started spreading throughout her body, wreaking havoc wherever they settled.

The cancer had been diagnosed on a routine Pap smear two years earlier. Angela had gone to her gynaecologist for her annual check-up, and neither he nor she had even considered that there might be a problem. They had briefly discussed her contraception, and Angela had told him that she and Andrew had decided that they would start trying for another child the following year. Her gynaecologist had done her smear and had reassured her that everything looked fine.

Two days later, at seven fifty-two in the morning, Angela's phone had rung. She had been about to leave the house to take Ethan to school. She had had his school bag in one hand and her keys and sunglasses and phone in the other and had awkwardly lifted the telephone to her ear. It was her gynaecologist, and Angela knew immediately that there must be a problem because he didn't phone with normal results. His motto was: 'If you don't hear from me, everything's fine. No news is good news.' This was supposed to be reassuring, but all of a sudden it had quite the opposite effect. There were some abnormalities on her smear, he had explained, and he had asked her to come in, with her husband, as soon as possible to discuss them with him. She had asked her gynae how bad it was; told him she needed to know and that she didn't care that he would be giving her the information over the phone; told him that if he didn't tell her, she would presume the worst anyway. That was the first time that he had mentioned the word *cancer*.

Angela had heard the phrase *her heart sank* before. In the books that she liked reading, people's hearts were always sinking. Angela had thought it was a nonsensical description. How could someone's heart sink? It wasn't as though hearts floated around in people's bodies. But the sensation she felt when she heard the word *cancer* was exactly the feeling of her heart sinking. It was as though the core of her being was drowning, falling through her feet and being set loose into infinity.

Angela had managed to keep herself from crying while she took Ethan to school, while she kissed him goodbye and greeted his teacher, while she discussed the school fund-raising recipe book with one of the other moms, but on the way home she had had to pull her car over onto the verge because the tears had been too thick for her to see the road properly. She had pretended to be talking on her cellphone. The thought that she was an easy target for hijackers didn't cross her usually security-conscious mind. She had eventually been able to resume driving and had somehow arrived at her house without having caused an accident.

She had phoned Andrew to inform him of the appointment with her gynaecologist that was booked for later that afternoon. He had had meetings scheduled for the morning and she had told him not to cancel them, that there was no point in his coming home then, that it wouldn't change anything. There is no doubt that he would have postponed his meetings and come home if she had told him that she had cancer, and not just that there were abnormalities on her smear, but she had been unable to bring herself to say the word.

She had moved a chair to the window, next to where Clarissa was sitting in her wheelchair, and had wept for three hours. It had been strangely comforting having Clarissa beside her. She provided a human presence, a hand that Angela could grip, without asking for any explanations or making any judgements. After three hours, Gugu, her housekeeper, had come into the room with a cup of tea. 'It's time to stop crying now. Your kids need you to be strong,' she had said, handing Angela the tea and a warm facecloth. Angela had managed to halt the tears, but that impression of having had her existence emptied out of her remained.

Angela could still remember with absolute clarity every detail of the subsequent appointment with her gynaecologist, even though two years had passed. Her husband had been wearing a light blue shirt and smelt very faintly of sweat, as he did when he had had an exceptionally busy day at work. The smell had been comforting to Angela, familiar. Her gynaecologist had drawn pictures for them on a piece of paper, explaining various options and prognoses. He had shown them the histology report, but to Angela it appeared to be in a foreign language. She hadn't fully understood what the word *adenocarcinoma* meant. She walked out of her gynaecologist's rooms booked for a hysterectomy the following Wednesday. The first time that Andrew cried had been when they were in the hospital car park, sitting in the car before driving home, when he phoned his father with the news.

For the next two days, Angela had carried on with her life as usual, except that she had been unable to eat. She had taken Ethan to school and Clarissa to occupational therapy; she had played tennis and gone to her Pilates class as though nothing had changed. She convinced herself that she wasn't telling anyone about the cancer yet because it was none of their business, but in truth it was because as long the word remained unsaid, she could still pretend that it did not exist.

Instinctively, Angela had known the power of words. She had known that until she managed to formulate the words to describe her diagnosis, it would remain amorphous and unborn, something she could ignore. It was for that reason that she avoided seeing her best friend, because she knew that she would be unable to hide her condition from her. This was difficult, as her best friend was also her neighbour. Usually they saw each other three or four times a day; it was inevitable that they would bump into each other soon. It happened before Angela was prepared for it, but it is likely that even if she had been able to schedule the meeting, she would never have been ready for it.

Jen had knocked on the door and popped her head in to ask if she could borrow a cup of icing sugar for the cupcakes that she and her daughter were making. Erica had to take cupcakes to school the following day, she had explained. It was strange to Angela that she hadn't cried when she told Jen the diagnosis. She had told her best friend calmly and clinically, using medical terms that she must have picked up from her gynaecologist because she wasn't consciously aware that she knew them. Jen had cried and Angela had hugged her and reassured her that everything would be fine. It was a bizarre reversal of roles, but one that would occur with everyone that Angela told over the next few days. She, the victim, would become the comforter.

———•———

When Angela and Andrew had first fallen in love and had sat mapping out the route of their life together, they had decided that they would have four children. Their reasons had been different – in fact, polar opposites. Andrew had wanted four children because he had been an only child and did not want his children to have the same lonely childhood experience that he had had. Angela had wanted four children because she wished to emulate exactly her own busy, happy childhood. After the birth of Clarissa, however, they had both changed their minds.

Angela had had an easy pregnancy with Clarissa. She had not had morning sickness, her legs had not swelled, and she had not suffered from backache or heartburn or any of the other minor maladies of pregnancy. She had glowed. All of her blood tests and scans until twenty-eight weeks of pregnancy had been completely normal. Angela had been assured that her pregnancy was low risk and that she was carrying a normal, healthy little girl.

At the time that Angela was pregnant with Clarissa, it was very fashionable to have a home birthing experience facilitated by a midwife instead of having a traditional hospital delivery with a gynaecologist. Since Angela had been assured that she was at low risk for complications, when she was twenty-eight weeks pregnant she had said goodbye to her gynaecologist and had transferred her care to a midwife who had been recommended by a friend of a friend.

Angela had been very happy with the midwife. She had come to visit Angela at her own home and had listened to her stomach with a funnel-shaped object that picked up the foetal heartbeat. She had measured Angela's blood pressure and had felt her abdomen to check that the baby was fine. She had hugged Angela when excess oestrogen had made Angela tearful and had recommended Rescue Remedy and tissue salts to calm her down. When Angela had asked her about further scans, the midwife had reassured Angela that they were not necessary and that women had delivered healthy babies for thousands of years without modern radiology techniques.

What Angela did not know, and what the midwife failed to pick up on her abdominal palpation, and what a scan at thirty-six weeks would have detected was that Angela's baby was lying breech. This was discovered only during the birth, when the midwife delivered a foot instead of the infant's head. The result was a protracted and very painful labour during which Angela tore extensively and her baby was starved of oxygen. The widespread damage caused by the lack of oxygen to the infant's brain left Angela's baby with severe cerebral palsy.

It took four years before Angela and Andrew found the courage to consider having another baby, and another three years after the birth of their second child for them to realise that they still wanted to have the four children that they had so long ago imagined having. Angela's diagnosis cut short that dream.

Initially, after the hysterectomy, it was the termination of her dream that bothered Angela more than the diagnosis of cancer. She grieved the perceived loss of her womanhood. It felt as though an essential part of her, that which made her female, had been removed. She discovered that she had unknowingly hooked an inordinate proportion of her identity on her ability to bear children. Later, after the oncologists had discovered that her cancer was invasive and she had started undergoing radiotherapy, that would all seem completely inconsequential.

———•———

Once the cancer had spread, in neat round cannonballs, to Angela's lungs and liver, and her doctors had started using the term *palliative* when planning her further treatment, Angela began keeping journals for her children. It became incredibly important to her that her children have a memento to remember her by; that in five or ten years' time, she would still be something tangible to them and not just an insubstantial memory. She wrote for Ethan and drew pictures for Clarissa. She realised that the pictures she was drawing for Clarissa – of the things that her daughter seemed to enjoy watching through the window: birds, buck, mongooses, the flowers in spring – had nothing to do with her specifically, but she hoped that somehow they would trigger in her daughter a remembrance of her mother. She understood that it would not be a concrete image of her, but was happy if it was just the emotion associated with mother that Clarissa re-experienced.

For Ethan, she kept detailed notes of what they had done each day. She wrote in his journal almost every night, so that the memories would be fresh and it would be more likely that she would be able to capture their essence accurately. She described to him how they had gone down to the San La Mer dam together and fed the catfish with breadcrumbs, and how the catfish had fought one another, flopping over each other in their greed for the bread, and how he had laughed at their antics. She wrote about the first time that Ethan slid down the fireman's pole on the jungle gym on his own, how proud she had been of him, and how he would drag her to watch weed-eaters for hours. The more aware Angela became of her mortality, and the closer her death felt, the more she wrote.

On the morning of Wednesday the second of November, the day before the murder of Advocate Norman Ware, Angela woke up feeling short of breath. It was a horrible feeling, a sensation of being unable to get enough air into her lungs, as though she was climbing a mountain at high altitude without having trained for it. Nevertheless, she got up slowly, dressed herself and then stumbled to the kitchen to make breakfast for her children and her husband. She insisted on these rituals, clung to them with the tenacity of a pit bull terrier even though they were so painful, because the routine created a semblance of normality. It was because her normality had been threatened, because she had experienced the chaos that existed if it slipped for even a moment, that she valued it so much.

She made scrambled eggs and toast for Ethan and Andrew. Clarissa struggled to chew and so Angela fed her a few teaspoons of strawberry yogurt. After breakfast, Andrew went off to work and Angela asked Ethan what he wanted to do that morning (she had taken him out of his preschool for the year in order to maximise her time with him). Ethan wanted to go down to the swimming pools and Angela decided to take Clarissa with them. Clarissa enjoyed being outside, and so even though it was difficult to move her, Angela made an effort to take her on outings whenever possible. Gugu accompanied her to help with the lifting and carrying.

Over the course of the morning, Angela began to feel more and more short of breath. Even minimal movement seemed to trigger wheezing. She gave up trying to splash with Ethan in the kiddies' pool, handing that over to Gugu, and went to sit down next to Clarissa. Heavy grey storm clouds were piling up in the previously clear sky and Angela felt a sudden sense of impending doom, as though something terrible was going to happen. She stood up to tell Gugu and Ethan that it was time to leave, but the effort was too much for her. She felt herself slipping, then fell inelegantly onto the grass.

From the shallow children's swimming pool, Gugu saw Angela collapse. She grabbed Ethan out of the water and ran across the grass to her employer. Angela looked so pale and frail, so completely broken, that Gugu was sure that she had died. Gugu's immediate reaction was one of panic. She told Ethan to sit still next to his sister and ran to the parking lot to find someone to help her.

The first person she caught sight of was Advocate Norman Ware. He was wearing a light blue tracksuit and looked as though he had been exercising, although when Gugu spotted him he was standing still, talking on his cellphone. Gugu hurried over to him and grabbed his arm, trying to pull him towards the pool area. The cellphone fell from his hand and hit the tarred ground, causing the screen to shatter, but Gugu, in her state of shock, was oblivious to the damage she had caused. Advocate Norman Ware was unable to decipher accurately Gugu's

petrified babble, but he understood enough to realise
that there was something dangerously wrong. He placed
his right hand on her left shoulder and looked her in the
eyes, urging her to take deep breaths and to try to calm
down. Gugu stopped wailing momentarily and Advocate
Norman Ware reassured her that she was doing well and
told her to explain slowly to him what the problem was.
His strategy worked and Gugu described how Angela had
collapsed and was now lying dead beside the pool. By
this stage, Gugu was trembling so much that Advocate
Norman Ware was concerned that she too might collapse.
He supported her with his arm as she led him to where
Angela lay. Neither of them noticed a silver Mercedes
driving past at the time.

Advocate Norman Ware soon established that it
was a false alarm: Angela was not yet dead. He called
an ambulance to take her to hospital and contacted her
husband to let him know what had happened. Gugu was
still trembling and shaking, and Advocate Norman Ware
doubted that she was in an adequate emotional state
to look after the children, so he waited with her until
Andrew Mallory arrived.

If Clarissa had been able to talk, she could have told
Gugu before she went to fetch Advocate Norman Ware
that her mother had not died. It was not yet Angela's
time to die. That would happen six weeks later, a few days
before Christmas.

Chapter Nine

DR DANIE VAN DEVENTER was a good forensic pathologist. If he made mistakes, missed something small here or there, it was because he was unreasonably overworked and not because he was incompetent or poorly trained. There might have been an element of frustration in his attitude, and he might have lost his temper a little too quickly when his assistants made elementary mistakes, and possibly he drank too much of the single malt whisky that he so enjoyed after leaving the mortuary on a Friday night, but all of that was to be expected, given the circumstances under which he was expected to work. His was not a job conducive to good mental health.

Advocate Norman Ware's body arrived at the Gale Street mortuary in the back of the unwashed white Forensic Pathology Services van in the early afternoon of Thursday the third of November. Before Dr Van Deventer could do the autopsy on Advocate Norman Ware, he had to complete post-mortems on two other murder victims who had come in earlier in the day (one stabbing and one gunshot); a suicide victim (hanging); and a victim of an accident between a taxi and a bus. The day was proving to be particularly busy.

Because of the plethora of popular television series

based on crime-scene investigations and forensic pathologists, the general public has a warped and far more romantic idea of mortuaries, especially South African mortuaries, than is actually the case. Real mortuaries are not populated by inordinately large numbers of beautiful people. There are not highly sophisticated laboratory facilities on site that can deduce within a couple of hours all sorts of miraculous things, such as the make of the nail polish with which the victim painted her toenails three months prior to her murder, or the country of origin of the strand of cotton caught in her stab wound. And the bodies are never as clean and plasticine-like as they appear on television. The stiff that Dr Van Deventer was working on when the delivery van dropped off Advocate Norman Ware's corpse, for example, had been lying in a muddy cane field for approximately four days before it was found. It had started putrefying and had become bloated and distended with gas. The skin covering the abdominal wall was tainted with a greenish tinge and maggots had taken up residence in the body cavities. Maggots were not the only creatures that had made a meal of the body; some of the victim's extremities had been gnawed off by cane rats. Naturally, if the producers of television programmes re-created reality down to such detail, they would lose viewers. Thus most of the general public continues to walk around with a perception of death that is far less disgusting than it actually is.

One other problem particular to the Gale Street mortuary in which Dr Van Deventer worked was that it was unable to cope both with the high volume of corpses that passed through it and with the large number of unclaimed bodies. It was equipped to cater for 120 bodies, but on the day that Advocate Norman Ware was brought in, there were 180 bodies in the mortuary. Ridiculously, some of the unclaimed bodies dated from 2008, three years earlier. The result was that staff had resorted to piling bodies onto stretchers and stashing them away in unused cooling fridges. It was in this environment that Dr Van Deventer was expected to perform his autopsies.

Some San La Mer residents, especially those who enjoyed watching popular forensic pathology television shows, might have imagined that particular care would be taken with the autopsy of Advocate Norman Ware, owing to his circumstances. That was not the case: Advocate Norman Ware's body was accorded exactly the same treatment as all of the other bodies on which Dr Van Deventer performed autopsies. He did not spend more time on Advocate Norman Ware's post-mortem, nor take more care with it or order more special investigations, just because the victim was wealthy and white and happened to be quoted regularly in various newspapers. In death, that was irrelevant.

At the end of the post-mortem, Dr Van Deventer had concluded the following:

1. Advocate Norman Ware was killed by blunt trauma to the head which had caused extensive intracerebral and extradural haemorrhages. The impression on his right temple was consistent with blunt trauma caused by the bronze cherub statue (Exhibit A).

2. The time of death was between 01h00 and 04h00 on 3 November 2011. This was based on the establishment of rigor mortis in the small muscles of the face, lower jaw, neck and wrists, as well as the body temperature and the colour and pattern

of lividity. Also of importance in determining time of death was the fact that the victim's stomach was empty. He was known, according to his wife, to have eaten a full meal of chicken stew at seven o'clock the previous evening.

3. The victim sustained severe mutilation. All the digits of both hands and feet, the nose, both ears, the lips, the penis and the scrotum, including the testicles, were likely to have been removed with a sharp, double-bladed instrument. There was extensive bleeding from the wounds, as evidenced from the crime-scene photographs and corroborated by clinical findings. Injury was likely to have been ante-mortem. Although these injuries were not the cause of death, they might have contributed to the speed at which the victim died and were highly suggestive of some form of torture.

4. The victim did not display any injuries consistent with a struggle or with attempts at self-defence. Obviously, since the fingers were absent, it was not possible to determine if skin from the killer was present beneath the nails.

5. Bloods were sent to the lab for a standard drug screen. Results are pending.

6. A malignant melanoma, 0.5 x 0.8 cm, was evident on the flexor surface of the victim's right wrist. Although no macroscopic secondary metastases were found, the melanoma was invasive on histology. This was an incidental medical finding and was unrelated to his death.

Had Dr Van Deventer been less busy and had he had more time to mull over the case, he might have concluded that the relatively minor trauma to the victim's head was not compatible with having caused the extensive cerebral haemorrhage that appeared to be the mechanism of death. There was no skull fracture present, and yet the apparent devastation caused by the blow was extensive. He should also have picked up that there was disproportionately little clotting at the amputation sites, even for an injury inflicted ante-mortem. He might then have wanted to know whether the patient was on blood-thinning medication, and, if so, how well controlled his INR and PTT were. On discovering that Advocate Norman Ware was not taking any medication, the question might have arisen as to whether he could have been poisoned. Dr Van Deventer might have included testing for Warfarin and other anticoagulants on the drug screen.

But Dr Van Deventer was busy and tired and was not inclined to look beyond the obvious.

———

Florence Magwaza had arthritis. She had arthritis in her knee joints, which creaked in the morning when she got up, and in her hips, which ached when she walked outside to the communal toilet, and in her wrists, on which she was no longer able to fit her watch. The arthritis was worse, however, in her fingers. Her knuckles were painful and bulbous, her fingers gnarled. On cold mornings, Florence could barely open her hands.

The arthritis in her knees and hips Florence could bear, but the deformity and restriction of her fingers and wrists were a problem because her livelihood depended on her being able to use her hands. Florence was a seamstress.

Florence had been taught to sew by one of the nuns at

the mission school near Ixopo that she had attended as a young girl. The nun had lived by two abiding principles that had guided all of her actions. The first was that the devil finds work for idle hands, and the second was that everyone should learn a skill. The result was that whenever the young Florence had finished her schoolwork, she was set to sew by the nun. The machine on which Florence had learnt to sew was a treadle Singer sewing machine. Florence had thought it beautiful, elegant even, with its shiny, curved black metal body emblazoned with the Singer name in gold. It had stood proudly on its wooden table base, like a ballerina frozen mid-dance. The nun had patiently taught Florence how to make tablecloths and napkins. Once Florence had mastered those, they had moved on to skirts and blouses and then, finally, dresses.

Florence had fallen in love with sewing, enjoying the textures of different materials between her fingers; the precision of feeding the fabric under the foot of the machine and of the neat little stitches that were formed on the other side; the rhythmic motion of her foot pushing down on the foot pedal. Unfortunately, Florence's sewing career came to an abrupt and unexpected halt. When Florence was sixteen, the mission school had been forced to close down and the sewing machines had sailed back to Ireland with the nuns. Florence had promised herself that she would find a way to sew again.

She had found a job as a domestic worker in Durban and had started saving money so that she could buy her own sewing machine. It was a slow process and life happened while she was trying to save. She fell in love, got married and had four children. Whenever it seemed to Florence that she had just about enough money to buy a sewing machine, something would happen that would require her to use her savings. It might be school fees for her children, bail for her husband, rent that needed paying or a new Primus stove that needed buying. Sometimes she had wondered whether God was trying to tell her that she was not meant to sew, and whether she was wasting her time and energy pursuing such an unlikely dream, but then she would remind herself that it was in God's house that she had first learnt to sew. It took her twenty years to save up enough money to consider buying her own sewing machine.

What Florence had not realised was that sewing machines had changed dramatically in the time it had taken for her to save up enough money to buy one. She had hardly recognised the machines that the salesman in the department store showed her. Where was the pedal? And the beautiful wooden table? The machines in front of her were white and plastic. They were not the elegant, immortal-looking machines that she remembered from her youth. She had left the store without buying herself a sewing machine.

The following day Florence had told her employer, for whom she had been working since she left the mission school and whose children she had helped to raise, about her great disappointment. Two weeks later, her employer had opened the back of her husband's silver 4×4 SUV to reveal a treadle Singer sewing machine precisely like the one that Florence remembered. Her employer had searched online and had found the machine advertised on Gumtree. She had bought it for Florence the same day. Florence had wanted to pay her with the money that she had spent so much time saving, but her employer had refused the offer. She had told Florence to spend the money on thread and material instead.

Another change had occurred in the years that Florence had been saving up for her sewing machine, one that Florence had not factored into her dream: the importation, on a very large scale, of cheap Chinese-made clothing into South Africa. Florence soon realised that it was not financially viable for her to compete with the Chinese goods. And so she kept her job as a domestic worker and, in her spare time, sewed for her own enjoyment. She made pretty smocked dresses for her granddaughters and shorts with elasticised waists for her grandsons. For herself, she made floral blouses and full skirts, and when her husband died, she sewed the black suit in which he was buried. It was a compromise that worked well until Florence's employer emigrated to Australia to be with her children and grandchildren. Florence was too old to find work now; no one wanted to employ a granny.

At the same time that Florence became unemployed, her daughter died of HIV, leaving Florence to look after her three children. Although she was upset at her bad luck, Florence had the grace to say a prayer of thanks for the nun who had taught her the importance of having a skill to fall back on in times of need.

Florence did not bother to compete with the Chinese sweatshops. She established a niche for herself altering clothes. If someone needed a hem to be taken up or a hole to be darned, they would visit Florence. If they had grown too big for a favourite shirt, Florence would carefully unpick the seams and eke out a millimetre or two on either side to make it fit. Likewise, if times were bad, Florence would take in a waistband, making sure not to cut the seam so that it could be adjusted again once there was more food on the table.

Florence learnt to be frugal. She preserved her scraps of material to use as patches or for appliqué work. She bought second-hand clothes from people and unpicked the seams to reuse the undamaged material. She saved the cotton from her tacking and used it over and over again. By taking these measures, Florence managed to make enough money to look after herself and her three grandchildren. Her arthritis threatened that stability. If Florence could no longer sew, she would have to support four people on her measly state pension, which was impossible.

One factor that Florence knew worsened her arthritis was the cold. If she could keep her joints warm, she could work, but when it was cold, it seemed as though her hands seized up and became completely immobilised. It was for this reason that Florence was most interested when she heard about the RDP houses that were being built in the area. The shack that she lived in was no barrier to the cold. The wind whistled straight under the tin roof and rain and damp seeped through the wooden walls. Perhaps if she lived in a proper house, with solid walls and a ceiling that did not let the rain in, the days that she was unable to move her hands would be fewer. That afternoon Florence went to the municipality and put her name down on the waiting list for one of the promised houses. She was not to know that the building of these government-subsidised houses would be plagued by corruption and incompetence.

———

Narges McIntyre was both beautiful and intelligent, a dangerous and powerful combination of qualities. Her mother was Armenian, and it was from her that Narges had inherited her thick, nearly black hair, her full and sensuous lips, her first name and her thirst for vengeance. Her father had been a Scot. From him she had inherited her acumen, her dogged perseverance and her surname.

Narges had worked hard at school and had achieved well. After completing matric, she had won a scholarship to the University of the Witwatersrand, where she had studied law. Once she had completed her honours degree, which she had done *cum laude* at Wits, she had applied to do her master's at Cambridge. Narges was firmly of the notion that an education was only fully completed by a degree at either Cambridge or Oxford. She was accepted into Newnham College and had stayed in Cambridge, first studying and then lecturing, for seven years. While she was overseas, Narges's parents had moved from Johannesburg to the Berea in Durban, where they bought and renovated a spacious old apartment with parquet flooring and big bay windows.

Towards the end of her seventh year at Cambridge, soon after she had applied to do her PhD, Narges received a telephone call from a physician at the St Augustine Hospital in Durban informing her that her father was in a critical condition in the intensive care unit after having suffered a major heart attack. Narges had bought an aeroplane ticket back to South Africa on the first flight that could accommodate her. She had landed in Johannesburg and caught the next flight headed to Durban. As she stepped out of the aeroplane, Narges hardly noticed the heat and humidity of the Durban air, so different from the English crispness to which she had become accustomed. She had hurried across the airport parking lot to the rental car agency and hired a dark blue

Volkswagen Golf. Narges had been driving up Argyle Road, past colonial mansions and tree-lined side roads, when her father passed away. She had been about seven minutes from the hospital.

Narges, who was unable to forgive herself for not being with her father during his dying moments, swore that she would not do the same thing to her mother. She moved into the fashionably revamped flat with her mother and started studying for her bar exam. She passed on her first attempt and accepted a position as associate professor in the law department of the University of KwaZulu-Natal. Apart from her work at the university, Narges shared chambers with a colleague who specialised, as she did, in commercial law. The university job provided her with intellectual stimulation and her private work provided her with a substantial income.

At the age of forty-six, Narges had never married. This was due not to a lack of suitable candidates, but to the fact that Narges had never had any desire to marry. She found the idea of marriage – of being bound and somehow subjugated to a man; of having to answer to someone other than herself – primitive and at odds with the principles of a civilised society. That is not to say that she had not had romantic relationships. Narges had had several relationships, some of which had even lasted a few years. Narges always ended them when they started to intrude on her independence.

Narges had never once experienced the broodiness so glibly described in women's magazines. She was indifferent to the ticking of her biological clock. On the whole, she found children to be clingy, whiny, usually sticky and most often, once they had grown up, disappointing to their parents, so she avoided having any contact with them and certainly never contemplated having any of her own. She had a dog, a captivating brown-and-white Jack Russell, and Narges was happy to bestow on her canine any latent feelings of motherhood.

At the time of the murder of Advocate Norman Ware, Narges's mother was still alive, although wheelchair-bound, and lived with Narges. Narges refused to hire a care assistant to look after her mother and saw to all of her mother's needs herself. She thought that this was only fair, since her mother had devoted a good fifteen years of her life to looking after Narges's every need. Narges had developed a slight paranoia about her mother's health since the death of her father and forced her mother to visit their family doctor for the tiniest qualm. This made Narges's mother feel like a hypochondriac, and she would spend most of the consultation apologising to the doctor for wasting his time.

On meeting her for the first time, some people would label Narges as hard or driven. Others, particularly men, would call her ambitious and career-oriented. Her beauty had the tendency to soften their adjectives. Psychologists might bandy about certain phrases when trying to analyse Narges, such as 'cluster A personality disorder' or 'low emotional quotient'. The truth was that none of these descriptions fitted her. Narges was a woman who knew precisely what she wanted from life and who worked diligently and persistently to ensure that she got it. Just because she did not display the normal range of emotions and feelings society expected of women did not in any way imply that she was not a compassionate, just and humane person. Narges was different, and the sheep-like mentality of ninety per cent of the population does not tolerate exceptions easily, which meant that Narges had few friends. It was her beauty that saved Narges, that made her acceptable and opened doors for her that would otherwise have remained closed, and Narges was fully aware of this. It was for this reason that she had decided, when she turned forty-six, to have a complete makeover. She had seen an advertisement for the Re!nvent Yourself clinic and had made an appointment for a consultation, which was how she came to meet Dr Phillip Landers.

Chapter Ten

DAMIAN VAN ROOYEN WAS not at his home in San La Mer on the night of the murder of Advocate Norman Ware. He was in a four-star hotel near Port Shepstone, on the South Coast. He had had dinner at the hotel – a fillet steak with pepper sauce and a side order of chips – and later on in the evening, at twenty-seven minutes past eleven, he had phoned the reception desk from his room and requested a wake-up call for seven o'clock the following morning. He had been in the hotel dining room eating breakfast at half past seven the next day, which was an hour and a half before the time that Advocate Norman Ware's body was discovered, and approximately three-and-a-half to six-and-a-half hours after the estimated time of death. He had a watertight alibi, which is why it was strange that he turned around and drove out of San La Mer immediately after noticing the police cars that had responded to the discovery of Advocate Norman Ware's body. He did not even get as far as driving past his home before he made a U-turn and retraced his route out of the estate. The most likely reason for Damian's abrupt departure was that he had a suitcase in the boot of his car that contained a drugged teenager.

———◆———

There are certain characteristics that are generally attributed to psychopaths: a lack of empathy; the inability to experience emotions in the same way that normal people do (psychopaths exposed to words such as *rape, murder* and *torture* do not show the same activity in the limbic area of their brain as normal people do; their brains respond in the same way to these emotionally charged words as they would to neutral words such as *tree* or *chair*); habitual lying and manipulation for their personal gain; semantic aphasia, or difficulty with properly integrating the emotional and language components of their thoughts; impulsivity; a low tolerance for boredom; egocentricity and grandiosity; and remorselessness. There are also certain childhood indicators that can predict the potential for adult psychopathy. These include sadism, usually expressed as cruelty to animals; pathological pyromania; compulsive lying, not necessarily for a discernible reason; truancy; and aggression towards or manipulation of peers.

Although Damian van Rooyen did not possess every single one of these qualities, many of them were recognisable in his behaviour. As a child, Damian had not specifically been cruel to animals, but he had physically and emotionally tormented his twin sister. The result of his sadism was that, at the age of fourteen, she had had to be admitted to a psychiatric unit in a state of catatonia resulting from severe depression and anxiety. Damian's compulsive lying and expert manipulation of those around him started in childhood and continued into adulthood. He felt absolutely no anxiety or fear while lying and was adept at changing his story to fit in with new facts as they were discovered. He was so unflappable, so convincing in his lying, that those interrogating him would often find themselves questioning the facts.

Damian worked as a computer systems analyst for a large corporate bank. He found his job boring and spent most of his day hacking into accounts and stealing money (it was as a result of this alternative income that Damian was able to afford to live in San La Mer). His colleagues disliked him – he was manipulative, arrogant and dismissive – and his boss was too cowed by Damian's psychological bullying and mockery to report his behaviour to the human resources department.

Damian considered himself to be far more intelligent than he really was. He had done a questionable online intelligence test which put his IQ at 148, something he seldom failed to mention in conversation. In fact, his intelligence quotient was closer to 105. He blamed the fact that he had dropped out of university on his lecturers, who he believed had been jealous of his intelligence. He was subsequently dismissive of university studies and university degrees. He completed a certificate in Microsoft software engineering that he claimed was far more challenging than any degree programme.

Damian had had a few girlfriends, but none had remained in a relationship with him for longer than a couple of months. He was dismissive of the women he dated, certain that none of them was clever or attractive enough to be justifiably going out with him, and he was incapable of fidelity. Damian's friendship circle consisted entirely of those people whom he was able to manipulate for some personal gain, financial or sexual.

Damian's initial attempts at killing were roughshod

and somewhat sloppy, although never enough so to have got him caught. He began toying with murder when he was eighteen. His first victim was an elderly lady who lived several streets from his parents' house in Melville, Johannesburg. He chose her purely because he knew that she lived alone, so the crime would be relatively simple to commit, and because he could see no real purpose for her being alive. His killing time was carefully chosen: mid-morning on a Wednesday, when he was supposed to be at school and when the streets were quiet. He was confident that he would not be caught, but was also reassured by the knowledge that if he needed an alibi he could bully one or two of his classmates into vouching for him. The mechanism of murder that he chose was simple, nothing nearly as fancy as what he would have developed by the time he moved to San La Mer. He taped the woman's mouth closed with some packing tape that he had brought along with him in the pocket of his tracksuit top and strangled her with one of her nylon stockings. Although the murder was amateur and experimental, it proved an epiphany for Damian. While watching the old lady's life slip away, he experienced an intensity of emotion that he had not imagined possible. It was a blend of arousal, headiness and exhilaration that left him on a high for weeks.

This raises the question whether psychopaths kill because it is only in performing such an extreme act that they are able to feel the depth of emotion that normal people feel when, for example, falling in love or achieving a long-term goal. Studies have shown that psychopaths have areas of the brain that are not as fully developed as those of normal people, specifically the amygdala and the uncinate fasciculus. They also have less grey matter in the prefrontal cortex. Is it these aberrant neural pathways, these short circuits in their brains, that cause their emotional blunting; that drive them to pursue ever-increasing stimuli in their search for pleasure; and that allow them to remain untouched by the consequences of their hedonism?

Damian found that his second killing, that of a homeless man whom he had lured to a deserted house with the promise of money, left him feeling slightly dissatisfied. It did not provide him with the same rush of endorphins that his first murder had. His third killing, performed exactly eighteen months after his first, left him bored and untouched. Damian realised that he would have to make his killings more elaborate, add more risk and excitement to them, if he wanted to remain fascinated and aroused by them, and he would have to push each one further than the last, ensuring that his murders became exponentially more extreme. Eventually, his murder ritual would become a complex composite incorporating aspects of a hunt, a theatrical performance and an intricate game of hide-and-seek.

Damian's initial three victims were selected at random, unfortunate casualties of chance and opportunity. They were all people on the outskirts of society, whose disappearance was unnoticed or expected. His fourth victim was very different.

Sasha-Lee Perkins was in Grade Eleven at a private girls' school in Pretoria. She was an all-round achiever. She was captain of the under-eighteen netball team and sang in the school choir; her marks were good (she was placed in the top ten of her class); and she was active in both the drama and music societies. Sasha-Lee wanted to study physiotherapy when she left school. Although she was not strikingly beautiful, she had an attractive, open face and her bone structure was good, and had she not been killed, she would probably have aged well. Damian picked her by searching the school website, which had an extensive photo gallery depicting different functions and events hosted by the school. Because Sasha-Lee was such an active scholar, she featured in many of the photographs.

Why did Damian choose that specific profile – that of a high-achieving, well-behaved, popular teenage girl – for all of his future victims? One has to wonder whether there was something in his past that had created antagonism towards this type of girl. Had he been rejected or ridiculed by such a high school sweetheart? Was he filled with pent-up rage and a burning desire for revenge? The answer to both questions is negative. Damian chose the profile of his victim according to how much and what kind of publicity it would accord him. He knew that public sympathy for well-behaved, attractive teenage girls would be high, which would in turn raise his profile. He had no interest in killing men or boys, because he preferred not to be labelled a sexual deviant, nor in killing prostitutes or drug addicts, because he felt that there was always an element of blame in the public's sympathy for them. His choice of class of victim was cold and calculated and devoid of emotion.

Damian stalked Sasha-Lee for a month before abducting her. To his surprise, he found the stalking almost as stimulating and empowering as the actual killing. It had a voyeuristic quality that he appreciated. Once he had kidnapped Sasha-Lee, he kept her tied up in his two-bedroom flat (he had moved out of his parental home by then) for three days before slitting her throat. Her helplessness, her alternating bouts of resistance and submission, her whimpering and crying and pleading, her inability to control her bowel and bladder, fascinated him. This was the perfect foreplay to the orgasm of his killing.

Over time, Damian embellished his methods. He devised creative ways of torturing his victims for weeks before killing them. He refrained from raping them but he sliced off their breasts, which he then sent to their families. He liked the implication of sexual assault that it suggested. Each killing became more elaborate, and it was on this fact that the police were hanging their hopes of catching him. They knew that eventually he would slip up in his attempts at showmanship.

By the time that Advocate Norman Ware was murdered, Damian had established a killing pattern. Approximately every three months, he took a two-week break. This was possible because he had conned his boss and his doctor into believing that he had chronic fatigue syndrome, which required significant rest time. Over these breaks he stalked and abducted his victims. He made sure that his locus operandi was different with each victim, although he didn't venture beyond the borders of KwaZulu-Natal. He would drug his victim and bring her back to his house, in which he had constructed an elaborate torture chamber. He would kill her once he was bored with torturing her.

All of this was possible because of the location of Damian's house. Damian had not chosen to buy a house in an isolated, rural area, because that would have been too obvious had the police decided to search for him. Instead, he had chosen to buy a house in the expensive San La Mer estate. He could afford to purchase a house there because of the money he had pilfered from the bank accounts of his company's clients.

An exclusive security estate offered the ideal place from which Damian was able to conduct his activities. First, the estate called itself an eco-estate, which meant that many of the houses were situated within protected green belts. Damian bought such a house so that he could bury his bodies in the indigenous forest surrounding the house, where they were unlikely to be disinterred by any eager landscapers. The only two problems – that of the stench of a rotting body and that of wild animals (they have a tendency to dig up bodies) – he overcame with a stroke of genius. Before burying the bodies, he drained them of their blood and preserved them in formalin. This prevented them from smelling and acted as a deterrent to the wild animals. The second reason a security estate was the perfect location for his hide was that it was not subject to the normal intrusions on a suburban house. He would not be interrupted by uninvited guests, because no one could visit him unless he gave them an access code. There would be no television licence officers or census officials or Jehovah's Witnesses who would come knocking on his door. He was assured of absolute privacy.

The third benefit of living on such an exclusive estate was that the police seldom made their presence felt, unless it was for the protection of a dignitary. The kind of wealth required to own a house on the San La Mer estate was seldom acquired through purely legal means, and so there were many residents who paid dearly to ensure that police presence on the estate was kept to a minimum. All of these factors suited Damian's purposes completely, which was why it was mildly irritating to him when he saw police cars and forensic vans swarming all over San La Mer.

Because Damian had been away, he had no idea

that Advocate Norman Ware had been murdered. He immediately presumed, on seeing the strong police presence in the estate, that they were there as a result of him. Damian was prepared for this eventuality. The constant possibility of being caught was part of the thrill that peppered his killings. A couple of months previously, he had bought a fake identity document for four thousand rands from a Nigerian who worked outside the Home Affairs office in Tongaat. He could have bought a cheaper one, but that would have given him the name of Bongani Zama, which even the persuasive Nigerian had thought would be inappropriate. So he had bought the more expensive green book, which identified him as Adrian Parker.

It took Damian a few minutes to reach the N2 highway from San La Mer after he had done his about-turn and left the estate. He travelled along the N2 for a couple of kilometres and then took the turn-off onto the N3. He drove until he reached the outskirts of Johannesburg in the early evening. He dumped the car, with the suitcase still in the boot, at a deserted scrapyard. Sixteen-year-old Corine Mouton, who had slipped peacefully from her drugged state to death at around the time that Damian drove past Harrismith, might have thanked Advocate Norman Ware in heaven for saving her from a far slower and more painful death.

Damian van Rooyen existed no more. His bank accounts were closed and his credit cards were found discarded in a rubbish bin by a vagrant. His boss, who was secretly relieved that Damian had never come back to work after his two-week sick leave, wondered where he was, but declined to report his disappearance to the police. Damian's colleagues didn't care. His parents, to whom he had not spoken for fifteen years, were unaware that he was missing. Snakes, spiders and birds took occupation of his house in San La Mer. Cobwebs covered his metal gurney like a shroud. His torture instruments became stained with guano and draped in fine, crackled snakeskins. The only person who noticed his absence, and cared about it, was Noluthando Gwala, but it was hardly appropriate for her to report it to anyone. Besides, she cared about his disappearance for entirely the wrong reasons.

Chapter Eleven

OWNERSHIP OF THE BRONZE cherub that had been used to kill Advocate Norman Ware was not difficult to trace. Detective De Villiers had sent an email to all the art dealers in and around Durban, with a photograph of the statuette attached, requesting any information on the item. He received a reply to his email within four hours. The bronze cherub had been imported by the owner of the Artsphere gallery at the beginning of 2010. The gallery had sold it six months later, for R284 000, to a Mr VJ Maharaj of 36 Seaview Drive, Umhlanga Rocks. Detective De Villiers nicknamed the statuette 'Cupid', although its official name, he discovered, was *Winged Angel of Unrequited Love*.

Number 36 Seaview Drive was a large and imposing house set behind high walls and a sturdy automatic gate. Detective De Villiers parked his hatchback on the verge and got out to ring the bell on the intercom. It was answered by a domestic worker who, convinced that Detective De Villiers was a criminal posing as a police officer, refused to buzz the gate open for him until after he had shown her his badge from over the top of the gate. It was probably not so much the visual of the badge that had eventually prompted the domestic worker to let

Detective De Villiers in as it was his threatening to arrest her for obstructing the course of justice.

The garden was well maintained and a short paved path took Detective De Villiers to the front door. Two triangular flags, one yellow and one red, fluttered on the end of bamboo rods in the northeaster. The housekeeper had opened the front door and was waiting for him at the entrance to the house. She wore a light blue housecoat, a frilly white apron and a matching blue-and-white mob cap. Detective De Villiers wiped his boots on the mat at the front door and followed the housekeeper into a spacious open-plan lounge.

It was immediately obvious that no expense had been spared in the decoration of the house. The floors were travertine adorned with luxurious Persian carpets. A feature wall was covered in gold embossed wallpaper and expensive-looking artworks hung from most of the other walls. Detective De Villiers suspected that Mr Maharaj must be well known at Artsphere. An ornate crystal chandelier twinkled from the ceiling and reflected off the supersize plasma-screen television strategically placed on the other side of the room in front of plush oxblood leather couches.

Mr VJ Maharaj met Detective De Villiers in the lounge. He was a short, middle-aged man whose jewellery – a thick, gold-chain necklace, a gold and ruby signet ring, and several chunky gold bracelets – competed for attention with his sense of self-importance. The top few buttons of his maroon silk shirt were undone so that his double chin could rest more comfortably between his neck and chest. He neither sat down nor invited the policeman to sit. His attitude was one of irritation and his body language made it clear that this was to be a short interview. He asked Detective De Villiers abruptly what he wanted and mentioned that he could not be long because he had a one-on-one meeting with the KZN premier later that morning. His attempt at intimidation had little effect on Detective De Villiers, who would not have taken any less time with his interview even if Mr Maharaj had had a meeting with the president later that day. His interest lay not in pandering to VJ Maharaj's whims, but in getting Advocate Norman Ware's murder investigation closed as soon as possible. The reason for this was that the case had the potential to escalate into a media feeding frenzy. The murder of a wealthy, well-known advocate who had had his genitals brutally amputated was guaranteed to be a front-page story. Detective De Villiers had been firmly warned by his superior that this was not to happen, as a significant proportion of the unofficial police budget was derived from bribes from San La Mer residents who wanted to ensure that neither investigative journalists nor the police had too much to do with the estate.

Detective De Villiers took a colour photocopy of the photograph of the bronze cherub, labelled Exhibit A, from his pocket, unfolded it with purpose and showed it to Mr Maharaj. It was at the moment that the photocopy of the murder weapon was revealed that Mr Maharaj proved what a proficient politician he was: his agitation lasted for only the tiniest fraction of a second before it was replaced by absolute charm. That instant of disquiet would probably have been missed by anyone other than Detective De Villiers, as would have been the pinprick beads of sweat that popped out on Mr Maharaj's forehead, even though the room was pleasantly cooled by ducted air conditioning. His meeting with the premier seemed to be forgotten as he ushered Detective De Villiers to one of the leather couches and intimated that he should sit down. He shouted for the housekeeper and offered the policeman a drink, anything he wanted, even Johnnie Walker Blue. Detective De Villiers requested a glass of Coke, and within a minute the housekeeper had placed the soft drink on a lacquered coaster on the glass coffee table. Detective De Villiers sipped slowly at his drink, wondering whether Mr Maharaj was aware of how indicative his change in attitude was. Years of detective work had given Detective De Villiers a certain proficiency in reading criminal behaviour. Had he been asked, he would have been able to predict accurately the aggression that Mr Maharaj would later display during his questioning. It was the typical defensive response of a guilty conscience; however, by the end of the interview Detective De Villiers was not sure what exactly it was that Mr Maharaj was guilty of.

Being a professional who liked to do things by the book, Detective De Villiers had with him a pocket voice recorder, which he laid out on the table next to his glass of Coke, and on which he recorded his interview with Mr Maharaj. The transcript of the interview is as follows:

Det. D.V.: Have you seen the statue before? The one that is displayed on this photocopy [refer Exhibit A].

V.J.M.: Do we really have to go about this in such a formal way, with the recorder and everything, I mean? It's just that it doesn't seem very necessary to me. Why don't we just have a chat, man to man, about some things?

Det. D.V.: I'm afraid that would not be possible, Mr Maharaj. I repeat: have you seen this statue before?

V.J.M.: I'm sure that you're aware, since you're such

a good detective and all, that I'm a very wealthy man. It might be to your benefit if we turn off that recorder and have a chat. Just a small chat, that's all that I'm suggesting. I mean, what do you think this is that you need a voice recorder? An American television show? *CSI* or something?

Det. D.V.: We have evidence that you purchased this bronze statue from the Artsphere gallery on [rustle of papers] 14 June 2010.

V.J.M.: So why are you asking me if I've seen the statue before? You seem to know that I have. You sure you know what you're doing here?

Det. D.V.: When did you last see this statue?

V.J.M.: If you insist on making this interview formal, then you're going to have to question me when I have my lawyer with me. I'm not going to answer any more questions without my lawyer present.

Det. D.V.: That's interesting.

V.J.M.: What's interesting?

Det. D.V.: It's interesting that you're asking for your lawyer now, because a minute ago you were accusing me of acting like I was on a television show. Now you're the one acting like you're on *CSI*.

V.J.M.: Don't you try to intimidate me. I know my rights. I refuse to say another word until I have my lawyer present. Just remember that I'm well connected. You can get into big trouble for harassing me like this. I am a personal friend of the chief of police. I can make sure you never investigate another case again.

Det. D.V.: I'm just trying to establish when you last saw the statue. People who are innocent usually don't ask for their lawyers to be present, or throw around all sorts of threats, when a policeman visits to ask them a few simple questions.

V.J.M.: Don't you try to trick me into talking. I'm saying nothing until I have my lawyer with me. This interview is over. Do you think you can find your own way out or should I call my domestic to show you out?

Det. D.V.: I don't think this interview is quite over yet. At present you're the owner of a murder weapon. I tried to do this the nice way, but if you're not going to cooperate, we'll have to take you in.

V.J.M.: I'm sorry? What did you say? A murder weapon?

Det. D.V.: Yes, what did you think I was here for? The statue that you bought eighteen months ago was used to kill a man two days ago. Now, will you please tell me when you saw the statue last?

V.J.M.: So you're not from SARS? You're investigating a murder? Sorry, I misunderstood what was going on here. If the statue was used in a murder, of course I'll help as much as I can. That's terrible, just terrible. Such a beautiful piece of artwork.

Det. D.V.: So when last was the statue in your possession?

V.J.M.: Unfortunately the statue was … was … stolen from me soon after I bought it. About a month after I bought it. I haven't seen it since then, I swear.

Det. D.V.: And you obviously reported the burglary?

V.J.M.: No. No, I didn't. You know, I didn't think it was worth wasting police time with. It wasn't like it was murder or anything and I know how overworked you guys are.

Det. D.V.: I see. So what exactly were the

circumstances under which this statue was stolen?

V.J.M.: I don't see why that's important. I had nothing to do with the murder. I wasn't even here two days ago. I was in Cape Town. You can check out my alibi. I was at a congress at the Cape Grace Hotel. You can check. I only got home late last night.

Det. D.V.: Is that right? I'm still interested in the so-called robbery of the statue. We'll be getting back to you with further questions.

V.J.M.: You'll be hearing from my lawyers. I guarantee that.

Det. D.V.: I expect we will.

End of transcript.

Detective De Villiers left Mr Maharaj's house confused. There were two things that bothered him, two inconsistencies in Mr Maharaj's story. First, no matter how much money one had, the theft of an object worth nearly R300,000 would always be reported, even just for insurance purposes, unless there were suspicious circumstances surrounding its theft. Second, Detective De Villiers did not often see relief on people's faces when he mentioned that an item that they owned, or had once owned, had been used as a murder weapon. Not unless it had been used for something else equally illegal.

————

The initial impression that Dr Phillip Landers left on Narges was one of disgust. Not only did she find him physically repulsive, with his oily, pockmarked skin, his squidgy little piggy eyes and his skew teeth, but his lecherous attitude was almost more repugnant than his appearance. She walked out of her first consultation with him convinced that she would never allow the man to operate on her. So how did she end up not only paying Dr Phil to do a rhytidectomy, breast augmentation, liposuction, abdominoplasty and vaginoplasty on her, but also sleeping with him? The answer is not simple, and what happened was probably the result of a combination of various factors.

Two weeks prior to Narges's appointment with Dr Phillip Landers, she had broken up with her boyfriend of two years. She had written an email to him outlining her rationale in ending their relationship. The reasons she gave included the fact that she no longer found him physically attractive, that his conversation had become tedious to her, and that she believed he lacked ambition in his career, which irritated her. He had written back to her – an emotionally charged and heart-wrenching letter, not email – accusing Narges of being shallow and materialistic, slating her for her obsession with her job and her inability to form lasting relationships, and calling her an egotistical and judgemental pseudo-woman. In no other of Narges's past relationships had she ever received such a response to her attempt to end things honestly and reasonably, and the letter from this most recent boyfriend threw her. She began to question whether there was any veracity in his accusations. For the first time in her life, Narges was forced to do some soul-searching and she was not entirely happy with the results. It was while she was in this state of emotional fragility that she had her first appointment with Dr Phil.

Had Narges not just recently received an accusatory letter from an ex-lover, and had she not been an emotional leper at the time of her initial consultation with Dr Phil, she would not have doubted the first impression that he made on her and would have cancelled all further appointments and rescheduled with another plastic surgeon. However, after getting home from the consultation, over her fifth cup of coffee for the morning, Narges was dismayed to realise that she disliked Dr Phillip Landers for exactly the faults for which her ex-boyfriend had accused her of being intolerant. She found herself horrified that she had judged the doctor, both personally and professionally, on his unfortunate appearance. And perhaps what she had taken for a lecherous leer was, in fact, a reflection of her own disproportionately inflated ego. Narges was so horrified with the terrible truths that she believed had been revealed by her soul-searching that, had Phil Landers phoned her at that moment and asked her to have sex with him, she would probably have agreed to, if for no other reason than to prove to herself that she was not as insubstantial as she recently had come to believe. Unluckily for Dr Landers, he did not phone her right then, and it would take him a bit more work and expense to get her eventually into his bed.

All of Narges's subsequent interactions with Dr Phil were tainted by her self-doubt. The more disgusting and slimy that Narges found him, the more she would berate herself for being shallow. The more her intuition screamed at her that he was of dodgy moral fibre, the more Narges believed that she was being too judgemental. When Dr Phil took a little too long to examine her breasts, and massaged them a little more tenderly than was clinically indicated, Narges thought that her inflated ego must have been imagining things. And when Dr Phil eventually invited Narges out to dinner, she felt obliged to accept the invitation, in case by refusing she was reinforcing the superficial and materialistic motivations that had driven her behaviour in the past. Such is the danger of self-examination.

Narges and Phil's first date was at the upmarket restaurant of a boutique hotel. Phil had booked a table outside on the veranda, and the sound of the waves crashing on the nearby shore formed the soundtrack to their liaison. After seating Narges and Phil, the waiter brought them a wine list and Phil selected an expensive bottle of champagne to begin with. Narges ordered the grilled calamari hors d'oeuvre and Phil chose the oysters. And if the overt way in which he winked when the plate of oysters arrived at the table, and the suggestive manner in which he slurped them from their shells, seemed lecherous, Narges attributed it to her rigidity and not to his coarseness. For their main course, they both ordered the langoustines. By the time the shellfish arrived, Narges was well on her way to becoming intoxicated. Getting drunk was not something that Narges, the archetypal example of a type A personality, habitually did; in fact, the last time that her alcohol levels were as high as they were at the time of the arrival of the langoustines was sixteen years before, at her thirtieth birthday party, when she had not realised that the celebratory punch that her friend made for the party was alcoholic. The reason she was sipping the champagne as though it were water, or non-alcoholic punch, was not that she particularly enjoyed champagne, or that her date was paying for it, or that she was having a fantastic evening. The reason Narges was drinking so recklessly was that she had discovered there was an inverse relationship between the amount that she imbibed and the obviousness of Dr Phillip Landers's faults.

By the end of the evening there was no better word

to describe Narges's condition than *smashed*. Had Phillip Landers been a decent gentleman, he would have taken her home and tucked her up in bed and left, but he was as far from a respectable person as Tehran is from Salt Lake City, so he drove her straight back to his house, where he proceeded to fuck her, with a little help from a blue diamond, no less than three times. The fact that Narges was semi-comatose did not seem either to hinder his progress or to bother him one iota.

The following morning, after waking up between the red satin sheets on Phillip Landers's bed, to the accompaniment of his intermittent grunts and snores, Narges tried to assess the extent of the damage. This was difficult because the night before was a nauseating blur. Narges's last clear memory was of eating a langoustine that appeared to have drowned in butter. It was rather an indictment of Dr Phil's lovemaking that Narges was aware of the fact that they had had sex because her recently tightened vagina was so painful, and not because of Phillip's sexual prowess. Narges gathered up her clothes and called a taxi to collect her. She left before Phillip Landers had arisen from his post-coital slumber.

Once Narges's initial shame had dissipated, and she had made a firm decision to resist any further soul-searching, she succumbed to anger. She considered whether there was any legal recourse available to her to nail Dr Phil. She also briefly considered asking the Nigerian ex-Olympic hurdler, who lived two flats above her, how much it would cost for her to take a hit out on Dr Phil's life, but she gave up the idea soon after the Nigerian was arrested for involvement in a drive-by killing. Besides, death would be far too quick and easy a way out for him. Narges had both patience and tenacity, two qualities that would ensure that she would eventually find a way to destroy Phillip Landers's life irreversibly. It was for this reason, and the fact that her vagina was still painful three days after her night of regret, that Narges had attended her follow-up appointment with Dr Phil Landers. She did not once mention their evening together while Dr Phil examined his handiwork, even though he made several suggestive comments that she ached to rebut. She allowed the full fury of the hard and cold light of Narges to shine on Dr Phil. And all the time, while he examined her and tried to chat her up or provoke from her a very solicited compliment of his lovemaking skills, Narges had been inspecting every detail of his consultation and his consultation room with the aim of finding something over which to take him down. Unfortunately for Narges, Dr Phil was not a bad surgeon per se, and so she had no grounds to sue him for negligence. Narges might have given up hope of having her revenge on Dr Phil had two things not happened immediately after her consultation with him. The first was that as she walked out of Phillip Landers's consultation room and observed him calling in his next patient, a skinny young thing with disproportionately large breasts, she realised that she was not the only patient who had been taken advantage of. The second was that she received her invoice for his surgery.

———◆———

Vincent Schreiber was frustrated in his job. He had been working for the *Sunday Times* for ten years and had not progressed beyond the portfolio of editor of the lifestyle section. He had endured ten years of interviewing minor celebrities about the details of their home decor, discussing recipes with chefs who had nothing more important to do with their time, and attending mind-numbing fashion functions that bored him. For ten long years he had been waiting for the break that would transform him into a features writer.

It was not only the mundane and tedious nature of his job that frustrated him, as he was in no way interested in home decor and fashion fads, but the stigma that it bestowed on him. He was always treated as though he was slightly inferior, as though, just because he wrote about anorexic models and interviewed interior designers for a living, he was unable to have a valid opinion on, for example, the passing of the Protection of Information Bill or the validity of Menzi Simelane's appointment as head of the National Prosecuting Authority. He was an avid tweeter, but he knew that his tweets never carried the clout of other, more prominent journalists. He threw his comments out into the ether, but he doubted that they reached many people. His great aspiration was to be re-tweeted one day by Gus Silber.

Schreiber had his own blog, called The Scribe, on which he was able to write and post the type of articles that he longed to author for the newspaper. He discussed current affairs and made political commentary; he analysed the economic situation and predicted a worsening of the recession; he ranted adequately and cynically about everything vaguely sentimental or clichéd. He tweeted links to new articles on his blog daily. Apart from its tendency to take itself a little too seriously, his writing was incisive and elegant and it was a pity that Schreiber had only five regular readers of his blog.

It was for the above reasons that when he was approached by Narges McIntyre with the suggestion that he follow up on certain investigations that she had initiated, he went home and got horribly drunk, by himself, on a bottle of Verve Cliquot that he had won at an award ceremony five years before and had been saving for the right occasion to open. This was the lead that he had spent his entire writing career waiting for.

Chapter Twelve

THE CONSTRUCTION OF THE RDP houses in which Florence Magwaza had shown interest had begun in the KwaMashu area, approximately thirty kilometres north of the Durban city centre. The land had originally belonged to the eThekwini municipality and had functioned mainly as a dumping site. It was not a remarkable piece of land: there were no sea views, only a view on one side of an industrial area and on the other of a township; it was in a dip and was hence lower than the surrounding areas, so any water tended to collect on the land, making damp an ongoing problem; and the air over it was permanently yellowish-grey from the pollution that was belched out by the factories in the neighbouring industrial centre. The land was probably suitable for nothing other than a landfill site, which was why it was odd that it was sold to a property developer, a Mr VJ Maharaj, on the twentieth of June 2009, for R1.4 million. Even odder was that within three months of the initial sale, it was bought by a company headed by a Titus Mokotla, for R6.2 million. This sale took place just as the property market had reached its zenith and was headed downwards.

Had anyone bothered to investigate, they would have discovered that Titus Mokotla, a councillor on the same eThekwini municipality that had originally sold the land, also owned a newly formed company claiming to specialise in the construction of low-cost and government-subsidised housing. VJ Maharaj was one of the company's board members. Regardless of the fact that it had yet to successfully build a single house, Titus Mokotla's company had won the tender to build RDP houses on the land. The tender was worth R300 million.

Construction of the houses had started towards the end of 2009, and the beginning had shown promise. Excavators and wheel loaders began rumbling over the land and dump trucks started moving earth about. Quantity surveyors stared through the little monocles atop their tripods and scribbled down readings, and areas of existing road were cordoned off. To all intents and purposes, it appeared as if the construction of the new houses was going full steam ahead. However, within two months of initiation of the building, rot, both literal and figurative, was starting to make its presence felt. Damp seeped up from the ground, ruining the establishment of any effective foundations. When the quantity surveyor on site mentioned this as a problem, she was told that there was not enough money to install an effective drainage system. This was, after all, low-cost housing. It is unnecessary to state the obvious here, that R300 million should easily have covered the construction of two hundred houses over and above the cost of any drainage systems that needed to be placed. It would have, had Titus Mokotla not been spending the money instead on luxury houses and cars, extended overseas gambling holidays and rare, auctioned Mafia memorabilia.

By May 2011, fifty of the two hundred houses had been finished. It was unlikely that any more would be completed in the foreseeable future, as funds had been exhausted. It was decided that the first fifty residents would be moved into the houses while Titus Mokotla waited for further government funds to become available to complete the project. Florence Magwaza's name had been selected from the waiting list of people who had applied for houses: she was one of the lucky fifty applicants who would be allowed to take ownership of their new house. Her name was chosen not because the developers had felt any empathy for her age and disabilities, or because they had looked into her background and found her to be a worthy person. They had chosen her from the 23,000 applicants because they knew that it would make for good publicity. Who would not support a government that provided a house to a kindly old lady who was single-handedly raising her three grandchildren by mending clothes?

<hr />

Florence Magwaza took extra care when dressing on Wednesday the eighteenth of May. She put on a dress that she had sewn for herself, a pastel-coloured floral dress with a fitted bodice, long sleeves and a full skirt. She wrapped a matching scarf around her head and completed the outfit with white stockings and the pair of pearly-cream court shoes that she had bought the day before from the Chinese shop. The reason Florence was making so much effort with her appearance was not only that she was moving into her new house on that day, or that she was going to be on television, on the SABC news, but that she was going to meet the president. Florence felt her heart bubble with joy at the thought that she, Florence Magwaza, was going to meet the leader of her beloved country. She imagined all of the things that she would ask him: about the struggle, and about how it felt to be the most powerful man in the country now, when his origins had once been so insignificant, and about what foods he liked best to eat.

The president, along with Titus Mokotla, the man whose company had built the houses, and a plethora of news reporters, was due to meet Florence at her shack at ten o'clock. The camera crew and reporters filming the episode for the seven o'clock news that night would then follow the president and Florence as a delivery van took her and her belongings to her shiny new RDP house. The finale of the publicity stunt would be a shot of the president handing Florence the keys to her new home. Florence was ready and waiting outside her shack at half past eight, when the first reporters and camera crew arrived.

Men set up lights outside her tin-and-wood house and wove themselves a cobweb of thick electrical cables. Florence had swept the small area of open ground in front of her shack prior to the media crew's arrival, but a man wearing a purple beanie scattered some pieces of paper and a couple of plastic cartons on the ground that she had earlier cleaned. A stray dog, a scrawny runt of a creature lying a few metres away from the action and peacefully licking his balls, appeared to cause great excitement among the camera crew. A woman fetched a few shortbread biscuits from the media crew's van and tempted the dog nearer to Florence's shack. Florence was not altogether happy with the turn of events, particularly since she knew that the dog was riddled with fleas and she had spent many an afternoon shooing it away from her home, but she felt too shy to complain and simply made sure that she gave the dog a wide berth.

The president's appearance was heralded by a fleet of sleek black cars made important with flashing blue lights. His bodyguards, all stocky men wearing black reflective sunglasses and wires from their ears, got out before the president and removed from the area anyone who did not have the requisite security clearance. This included the stray dog, which caused a furore among the media crew. Eventually, at three minutes past ten, the president emerged from his car. Florence smiled nervously at him and he smiled back at her, a broad, promise-filled smile that made Florence's heart lurch. The following moments passed in a haze of excitement and camera flashes, and by eight minutes past ten the president was getting back into his luxury car. Although Florence had done little more than smile at him, she was not disappointed. She understood that this was not the time for her to chat to him and offer him a cup of tea. That would happen later, when he opened the door of her new house for her.

Florence's desires were not to be fulfilled. She did not have time, once the delivery van had dropped her off at her new house, to ask the president what his experience of the struggle had been like or even to find out what his favourite food was, nor did she get the chance to offer him a cup of tea and a sugar biscuit from the batch that she had baked specially for the occasion the night before, and had kept with her in her handbag. She had been allowed to stand next to the president while he handed her a key (it hadn't been the real key to her house, but an oversized one designed to be readily visible by television viewers), and they had both smiled while the cameras flashed. The president had then said a few well-rehearsed words to the news reporters and had left in his black car, with the full brigade preceding and following him as though he were part of a military convoy. He had not even said a proper goodbye to Florence.

Once the president had gone, Florence's disappointment had budded into tears that dripped down her cheeks. The camera crew had been ecstatic. This was the emotion they were looking for. They filmed and photographed her extensively while she sat on the step of her new apricot-coloured house with tears running down her cheeks. One of the headlines that evening read: 'Tears of Joy at New House'. It was an inauspicious beginning to Florence's residence in her new home, and one that was in many ways representative of the spirit of the eighteen months she would spend in the apricot house.

———————

Although Elisma Ware was, by default, a suspect in her husband's murder (spouses always are, and she had been in San La Mer at the time of the murder), Detective De Villiers never seriously considered that she might have killed her husband. There were a couple of reasons for this. The first was that she was a little old lady, and little old ladies, in Detective De Villiers's experience, tended to kill their husbands by means other than blunt trauma to the head and genital mutilation. They preferred more elegant methods, such as poisoning or, in the case of absolute desperation, perhaps stabbing with a silver letter opener or shooting with a pistol with pearl inlays. The second reason Detective De Villiers did not suspect Elisma Ware of killing her spouse was that it was clear that she had loved and adored her husband. That she was completely devastated by his death was obvious and undeniable.

One of Detective De Villiers's assumptions was correct and the other was not. He was incorrect in presuming that Elisma Ware was a little old lady. She was only sixty, and had he seen her the day before her husband's death, Detective De Villiers would have described her as an active and well-groomed mature woman. Norman Ware's death had aged Elisma overnight. It was as though the tears that streamed constantly down her cheeks had worn furrows into her face, leaving her skin with the appearance of a crumpled piece of parchment. Her hair, which previously she had blow-dried and set every morning, now hung loose in limp ash-blonde locks. The weight of her husband's untimely demise forced Elisma's shoulders forward and rounded her spine and turned her usual stride into a shuffle.

The way in which Elisma Ware had aged since her husband's death seemed to be evidence of the authenticity of Detective De Villiers's second, and correct, assumption: Elisma Ware had loved her husband.

Norman and Elisma Ware had been married for six years at the time of his death, but Elisma had loved him for far longer than those six years of matrimony. Elisma had first met Norman Ware when she was thirty-one, and she never hesitated to tell anyone that it had been love at first sight. Well, her first sight, at least. The love had not initially been mutual. Norman had been married at the time and had been, unusually, very much in love with his wife. He had shown nothing more than professional interest in the eager new receptionist who had started working at his law firm in January 1984.

Elisma Ware could never have been described as beautiful. She was not unattractive and her features – although each one in itself was noteworthy: her eyes were a clear, light blue; her lips were well shaped and bordering on full; her nose was neither too large nor too small, neither too wide nor too narrow – appeared slightly unbalanced and disproportionate when put together to form a whole, so that her eyes were too small for her face and her lips too close to her chin and her nose slightly off centre. She did have one rare advantage to her appearance. Elisma Ware became more attractive as she aged. It was as though with time her features settled into her face and became comfortable with their positions so that, while at twenty years of age she would not have warranted a second glance, at forty she would probably have been rated as reasonably attractive. She was in the middle of her metamorphosis when she met Advocate Norman Ware, but it was not for her increasingly pleasing countenance that he fell in love with her.

Although Elisma claimed that she had fallen in love with Norman Ware the first time she saw him, it is more likely that her amorousness blossomed around the respect and admiration she developed for Norman's work. In a company full of unscrupulous rascals, Norman seemed, to Elisma, to be the only person with any substantial moral fibre. Norman had championed the lost causes. He had represented a researcher who wanted to take a large international pharmaceutical company to court over irregularities in the drug trials they were running. Norman took on as a client an obese man with end-stage diabetes who was trying to sue a well-known hamburger restaurant chain for his illness, and he represented a journalist who was facing ten years in jail for having blown the whistle on a corrupt politician. On occasion he even took on pro bono cases. Although Advocate Norman Ware did not rake in millions of rands for the legal firm in which he was a partner, he fulfilled a very important role: he was the firm's conscience. He was paid well to play this part, since it was not a popular job.

Elisma's respect for Norman was not limited to the integrity with which he handled his professional dealings, but was also inspired by the upright and honourable way in which he conducted his personal affairs. As the personal assistant to the firm's five male partners, Elisma was often given the delicate task of misleading a wife about her husband's whereabouts, or creating an alibi for an unaccounted-for night away, or even buying token gifts or flowers in apology to cheated-on partners. Norman never once asked her for such a favour. It was a bittersweet pill for Elisma to swallow that she so loved the way in which the man she loved, loved his wife.

For years, Elisma admired Advocate Norman Ware from afar. She observed him so keenly, through the door that separated his office from hers, that she noticed things that even his wife failed to notice, such as the first grey hair that appeared in his head of almost-black hair, just after his forty-third birthday, and the gradual, barely perceptible change in colour of the mole on the underside of his wrist from brown to reddish brown and then to blue-black, and that the skin beneath the small stainless-steel key that he wore permanently on a chain around his neck was a full shade paler than the surrounding sun-exposed skin. Over time, Elisma learnt what Norman's favourite foods were, and how he best liked to drink his coffee – Starbucks only, warm not hot, and with just a dash of milk, no sugar – and what size nib he preferred on his pens. She built up a complete memory bank: each of Norman Ware's preferences, likes, dislikes and desires was carefully sorted and filed away to be drawn on whenever the need arose.

Elisma never abused the information that Norman Ware had unwittingly fed her. Occasionally she might have made him a lunch of his favourite roast beef fillet sliced onto fresh white bread and smothered in wholegrain mustard and handed it to him at work, claiming that she had brought far too much to finish herself; or she might have purchased for him, after what she knew had been a particularly difficult week at work, a gift of a bottle of the Vergelegen Cabernet Sauvignon that she knew he so cherished; and often she baked him batches of her irresistible peanut butter biscuits and left them on his desk, packaged in brown paper and tied with raffia, along with a note that might have said something to the tune of 'for a boss who deserves a treat'. She never once used her knowledge to make a move on him or to try to win his heart, and if over time he developed for her an enduring and warm affection, it could hardly have been said to have been through any design or ulterior motive on the part of Elisma. The only action for which Elisma had felt any guilt, for which she had doubted her intent and for which she had occasionally asked forgiveness in her prayers was her purposeful use of a perfume which she had discovered, while she inadvertently overheard Norman Ware talking to a colleague, that Norman found to be irresistible and to which his wife was, sadly, allergic.

Although Elisma doted on Advocate Norman Ware and spent a large proportion of her time either thinking about him, or working late to be near to him, or involving herself in activities designed to make him happy, such as slow-roasting a beef fillet alone at home at night to offer him, sliced on bread, the following day, she did have other interests and hobbies that filled up her time. No one could have accused her of being a lonely spinster. Elisma enjoyed reading, especially historical biographies, and she was a founding member of one of the only non-fiction book clubs in the country. It was a select group of people, some of whom travelled from as far as Pietermaritzburg, that met once a month at the Ballito library, in a dusty fluorescent-lit side room. Elisma, as the chairwoman, would go in before the seven o'clock start of the meeting and set the portable wooden desks into a circle. It was around this circle that the books of the month would be seriously discussed and dissected. Only highly recommended red wine – John Platter four-star or above – was imbibed during these book club meetings. Membership was strictly by application and acceptance by majority vote.

As well as being a reader of historical biographies, Elisma was an avid collector of trivia and belonged to two different pub-quiz teams. One of the teams to which she belonged, named 'Les Quizerables', had been formed by Advocate Norman Ware at the time when San La Mer started holding pub-quiz evenings for its residents. Norman Ware had been short of a team member, since his first wife detested pub quizzes and refused to join him, and so he had invited Elisma to join his team. This was seven years before they got married, and he had not for a moment suspected that she would prove to be such a valuable team member. He also had no idea how much Elisma looked forward to these evenings with him, even though she still called him Advocate Ware around the quiz table. In order to ensure that she never got displaced from the Les Quizerables team, Elisma studied trivia. She watched shows such as *Who Wants to Be a Millionaire?*

and *The Weakest Link* and memorised the questions and answers from the game of Trivial Pursuit in order to make herself indispensable. The habit of collecting bits of trivia remained after she and Advocate Norman Ware got married, even though by then there was no chance of her being shunted off the team.

Elisma had never planned it to be the case, but when Advocate Norman Ware's first wife had been diagnosed with an aggressive form of muscular dystrophy that the doctors predicted would leave her dead in less than a year, it had been to her that Norman turned in consolation. There were those people who accused Elisma of poaching a dying woman's husband; those who misread her care as deviousness; and those who slighted the intention behind her actions over the previous decade. Such inferences were not the case, and if there had been any calculation behind Elisma's actions, it had been on a purely subconscious level (except, of course, for the perfume that she chose to wear). The more logical reason why Advocate Norman Ware turned to Elisma in his time of heartbreak and distress was that their relationship as employer and employee had always been one of care and respect, and that over the years Elisma had come to represent comfort and homeliness to Advocate Norman Ware. Her love for him had manifested almost as a mother's love, and thus it was natural that he should seek solace in her biscuits, and her familiar scent, and her knowledge of him, when his wife's life ended so tragically.

The last year that Advocate Norman Ware spent with his first wife was a difficult one. He was forced to watch the degeneration of her muscles; to observe, helplessly, as the disease progressively weakened her arms and legs, leaving her wheelchair-bound, and then moved on to her core muscles, rendering her unable to swallow or to talk. A feeding tube was inserted into her stomach, directly through the abdominal wall, through which Advocate Norman Ware fed his wife yogurt and vegetable broth. The last muscles to go were her intercostals, the muscles between her ribs. They rapidly wasted away, and with their increasing paralysis, Advocate Norman Ware's wife's breaths became more and more shallow, until eventually they stopped altogether. It would have taken someone with a heart of stone to have resented Norman Ware the one pleasure that he found in that year: the time that he spent with Elisma.

Neither Advocate Norman Ware nor Elisma made a conscious decision to increase the scope of their relationship from that of employer and employee to that of friends. It happened almost without their being aware of it, surreptitiously, in the odd meeting for a caffé latte after work at a quaint coffee shop in Morningside, or the occasional lunch together at the restaurant of a popular art gallery. There was nothing untoward in their relationship; no sexual undertone. Elisma understood exactly what Advocate Norman Ware was seeking: comfort, escape and companionship, and she provided it. She always carried with her, in her handbag, an interesting book and she would read passages that she had previously highlighted to Norman over a cappuccino or a chicken-and-cashew wrap. And so Advocate Norman Ware learnt, during his first wife's illness, that the ancient Egyptians believed in an afterlife on the Island of Reeds – a fertile, green and lush land surrounded by water – that the Greeks came to refer to as *paradeisos,* and from which the word *paradise* is derived; and that the southern ground-hornbill, as part of its mating ritual, looks for a food gift that he wraps in nest-lining material and presents to his prospective partner; and that the female praying mantis eats her partner once they have completed mating in order to optimise her strength for the process of reproduction. Some days, after lunch, they would wander around the gallery together and discuss the art. Their tastes were different: he liked the more abstract pieces, the triangles that appeared to be making love and the floating kitchen utensils; she liked the realistic works, the detailed portraits and landscapes. Norman Ware and Elisma's friendship sneaked up on them and it was only natural that it should continue, and blossom even more, after the death of his first wife.

To the casual observer, the scenario in which Advocate Norman Ware and Elisma found themselves after Norman Ware's first wife's death would seem particularly clichéd. The tale of the high-powered businessman running off with his secretary before his wife's body is cold in its grave holds a certain sordid predictability. It is the kind of story that, although common, gets repeated endlessly around bridge, coffee and dinner tables. Acquaintances seem to find a vindictive glee in the downfall of their compatriots. In fact, and contrary to their friends' and associates' beliefs, Norman Ware and Elisma's relationship was splattered with none of the usual indiscretions that typify the cliché. He had not run after Elisma for carnal pleasure, nor had he been having an illicit sexual relationship with her for years behind his unsuspecting and innocent wife's back. He had not lusted after Elisma's body (it was, after all, rather matronly and hardly worth lusting over) and she was not the requisite twenty years younger. Likewise, Elisma had not sold herself to Advocate Norman Ware for material gain. Their relationship was in no way constructed on either sex or money. Proof of this lay in the fact that their marriage was never formally consummated. Norman and Elisma Ware, in six years of marriage, had never had sex.

That they did not have intercourse does not imply in the least that they were not affectionate; that they did not hold hands and kiss each other on the lips and cuddle before falling asleep at night. But if, as it was, Norman and Elisma's relationship was so happy, so mutually fulfilling, so comfortable, why was it sexless? There is, after all, no unwritten rule that denies intercourse to those who marry after a certain age or precludes sex from a friendship. The answer is surprisingly simple. Elisma was a virgin. She had never had any desire for sex. The idea of sex slightly repulsed her. The thought of being so close to someone else, of sharing odours and bodily fluids and commensal bacteria with another person, seemed distasteful and unhygienic to her. Norman Ware, on the other hand, enjoyed sex immensely and had had a lively and experimental sex life with his first wife. They had shared and explored their sexuality for twenty years, and after her death he could not bear to share that intimacy with anyone else. It thus suited both Norman and Elisma to have a platonic marriage.

There was one stain on the perfection of Advocate Norman Ware and Elisma's relationship, one aspect to it, apart from its sexlessness, that would have worried any psychologist bothering to analyse it. There was never complete equality. The remnants of their past roles – those of employee and employer; adorer and adored; lover and beloved – still tainted, to some degree, all of their interactions. The balance of power was never quite centred. This was by no means the cause of Advocate Norman Ware's murder, but it certainly was part of the milieu in which his death occurred.

Chapter Thirteen

VINCENT SCHREIBER AND Narges McIntyre met for the first time at a chocolate bar in a busy shopping mall. Narges had suggested the venue. She had chosen it specifically because it was impersonal and public, and because she was premenstrual and had been craving chocolate. Vincent had not objected to her choice, and so they had met there at four o'clock in the afternoon on Thursday the fourth of August. There was an immediate and mutual attraction between Vincent and Narges. He had found her independence and ambition exceptionally sexy, and Narges had liked Vincent's cynicism and wry outlook on life. Eventually they would end up living together and, contrary to either of their paradigms or expectations, adopting a child orphaned by HIV, but they maintained a professional distance while they were jointly bringing about the downfall of Phillip Landers. Neither of them wanted to jeopardise their operation since it was equally important to both of them, for Narges on a personal level and for Vincent on a professional one.

During their initial meeting at the chocolate bar, Narges was completely open as she explained to Vincent the situation between herself and Phillip Landers. She did not allow anything that she might have felt for Vincent to interfere with the level of detail with which she described what had occurred between her and Dr Phil. Vincent nodded empathetically while she spoke, trying not to betray the fact that his mind felt compelled to imagine in graphic detail all that she was narrating. He was rather relieved when Narges reached the end of her story and moved on to the issue of the billing, on which Vincent was far more easily able to concentrate.

By the end of Narges and Vincent's initial meeting, four hot chocolates after first laying eyes on one another, they had established a plan of action to bring about the ruin of Dr Phillip Landers and the promotion of Vincent Schreiber. There were two elements on which they were basing their case against Phillip Landers. The first was that he was having unethical and inappropriate relationships with his patients, and the second was that he, along with the private hospital from which he was working and in which he had shares, was charging for services not rendered and products not used.

Narges had noted on her bill that she had been charged for a five-litre bottle of disinfectant and an entire reel of micropore tape. Had these both been used in the quantities stated, Narges should realistically have come out of theatre a mummy, preserved for eternity. There were numerous other examples of overcharging, and although the amount on Narges's bill due to overcharging was not significant on its own (it totalled a couple of hundred rands), if this quantity was added to every patient's bill it would work out to a considerable sum. Narges had questioned the receptionist about the quantities of various products claimed to have been used and had been told that the theatre staff opened a new bottle of disinfectant for each patient, and so needed to charge for a full bottle each time. Narges thought this was unlikely and suspected that the hospital used the same bottle of disinfectant for a hundred patients, while charging each one for a new bottle, and so had tasked Vincent with the job of checking the veracity of the statement.

Vincent's second job was to try to get other of Dr Phil's patients to admit that they had been sexually harassed by the doctor. This would prove far easier than the first job, as there were many disgruntled patients as well as patients' husbands who had visited Dr Phil's rooms.

Vincent Schreiber explored all possible avenues to obtain the information and proof that he needed to write a convincing, litigation-proof, front-page story. He interviewed theatre and cleaning staff, promising anonymity. He chatted up Dr Phil's receptionist – who was now quite amenable to being chatted up, having had her heart broken by Phillip Landers two days before, when he had told her point-blank that he had no intention of making her his wife – and teased valuable snippets of information from her. He made sure not to make it too obvious what he was after, because he did not want to risk offending the already vulnerable woman. He was needlessly cautious; had he simply told her what he was doing and asked her the questions he needed answered, she would have been more than happy to be complicit in exposing her boss's shenanigans. Her pride meant more to her than her job. But Vincent Schreiber was careful and did not want to take any chances that Phillip Landers might find out what he was after. The last approach that Vincent took to make sure that his story was watertight was to pose as a patient himself.

Although he was no Adonis, Vincent Schreiber was by no means unattractive. He had no outstanding features that obviously required plastic surgery: no bat ears, or trumpet of a nose, or hanging jowls. He researched possible procedures that he might plausibly request Dr Phil to perform, but none of them seemed suitable for him. He didn't want his fat removed from his waist and injected into his biceps, because he already had well-defined biceps from years of kayaking. His face was wrinkled, but not inordinately so for someone of forty, and thus it seemed ridiculous to him to go to Dr Phil requesting a facelift. Likewise, his full head of hair precluded an appointment requesting a hair transplant. It was a dilemma that he took to Narges. Although she would never have admitted it at the time, Narges was rather pleased that Vincent had no obvious deformities or faults needing plastic surgery. Eventually they decided that Vincent might ask Dr Phil to create a more pronounced abdominal six-pack for him. Thus it was that Vincent Schreiber found himself sitting between two human Barbie-doll replicas in the waiting room of Re!nvent Yourself.

Dr Phil was disappointed but curious when he called Vincent Schreiber into his consulting room. He had seen him in the waiting room but had presumed him to be a boyfriend or a husband, as he seldom had male patients. It was only when he picked up the file his receptionist had left on his desk that he realised it was Vincent who was the patient. Dr Phil's attitude with Vincent was completely different from that which he adopted with his female patients. Whereas he took his time chatting to his female patients and getting to know them before examining them, he requested that Vincent get straight onto the examination bed while simultaneously asking him what the problem was. He did a very cursory exam on Vincent, omitting all of the gentle massaging and sensual touching that characterised the examinations of his female patients. He had finished seeing Vincent within ten minutes and ushered him unceremoniously out of the room. Prior to his leaving, Vincent asked Dr Phil for a quote for the procedure, which Dr Phil promised to email him. Although Phillip Landers was not ecstatic about operating on a male patient, he was not about to give up the chance to make money. Stupidly, he thought that he would charge Vincent even more than he usually charged, almost as a form of compensation for his being male. Perhaps it was a surcharge in lieu of the sex that he invariably extorted from his patients.

Vincent left Phillip Landers's rooms disgusted. It was not only the man himself who disgusted Vincent, but the whole ethos of artificial youthfulness and plastic beauty that his practice promoted. It had not helped at all that Vincent was unable to look at the man without imagining him taking sexual advantage of Narges. There was some compensation, however. Vincent had come away from the consultation with the promise of an emailed quotation from Dr Phil and the telephone numbers of three disgruntled patients from the receptionist.

Vincent and Narges's case against Dr Phil, and the hospital from which he worked, was ready by the end of October. They were confident that the article Vincent was planning to sell to the *Mercury* and the *Daily News* was accurate, not open to charges of libel, and sure to destroy Dr Phillip Landers's medical career and personal life. Vincent knew that his research into the case, and his writing up of the lead article, would at last project him into the league of journalists to which he aspired, and Narges was certain that she was about to satisfy her lust for revenge.

The article was due to be published on the front pages of the widely read *Mercury* and *Daily News* on the third of November. On the second of November, at approximately midday, Narges phoned Dr Phillip Landers's landline at his home in San La Mer. This was not because she wanted to warn him about the article's imminent publication, or give him a last chance to acknowledge the wrong of his ways and beg forgiveness. Narges phoned with a purpose that was an integral element of her revenge. She specifically chose to call his home number because she knew that he was at work and so would not answer. She wanted to leave a message for him to come home to, preferably with an unwitting female in tow, once it was too late for him to do anything about his impending doom. The phone rang six times before clicking over to the automated voicemail that asked her to leave a message after the tone. Narges left a long message, claiming that he taken advantage of her and used her for sexual and monetary gain. She accused him of acting unethically and contrary to the principles of his profession. She coldly explained that she had ample evidence from numerous witnesses to bring him down, and that it would all be published the following day on the front page of the *Mercury*. She ended by telling him that she hoped that he had learnt his lesson.

The message was harsh and cold, the words those of a bitter and scorned woman, and they probably would have given Phillip Landers more than a sleepless night and an agitated stomach ulcer if Narges had left the voicemail message on Dr Phillip Landers's landline. Unfortunately, in her haste to get her revenge, Narges had pressed an eight instead of a five, and so Phillip Landers slept peacefully on the night of the second of November and awoke the following day blissfully unaware that his professional life was on the brink of collapse.

—◦—

The house that Florence Magwaza had so looked forward to inhabiting, and that had graced the front pages of newspapers and prime-time television screens, soon began to show evidence of its poor construction. The first fault that Florence noted was the damp that seemed to seep from the ground, making its way meticulously up the walls. It initially appeared as an ugly bubbling of the apricot paint. When Florence tried gently to clean the bubbles, the paint began to peel off completely, leaving the walls with a dirty, mottled-brown appearance. Soon mould began to grow over the areas of damp. No matter how many times Florence scrubbed the now bare walls with Jik, the mould returned. Florence might have put up with the damp and the mould, but she could not tolerate the layer of water that, soon after the damp appeared, began to leak up through the floor after heavy rains. It seemed to her that her house had been built on a river. Whenever it rained, or the clouds in the sky threatened rain, Florence packed her floor with newspaper to limit the water damage. It was an unsustainable situation.

Over the next few months, faults started blooming on the house in the same unexpected but almost predictable way in which flowers bloom every spring. A thick crack crept its way slowly from the bathroom window to the ceiling. One of the walls sank, leaving a gap of two centimetres below the ceiling. The wind whistled through this opening as sharply and unremittingly as it had done through the tin and wood of Florence's previous home.

On an evening in May, when the weather was beginning to turn cold, Florence closed a window and all the panes of glass fell out, shattering on the floor. It was too expensive for her to replace them.

Florence did not know what to do. She could not move back into her previous home, as it had long since been occupied by new inhabitants, but she could not afford the continual repairs to her current home, especially because her arthritis had flared up in the cold, limiting the amount of sewing she could do. She laid complaints with the municipality, waiting for hours in queues and filling in endless forms, but she was never rewarded with any sort of response to her grievances. Florence then tried to contact the builders who had built the house, but was informed that the company had folded. By now Florence was desperate. Her arthritis was crippling – she was barely able to get out of bed in the morning and every one of her joints ached continuously with a dull, throbbing pain – and two of her grandchildren had been admitted to hospital with pneumonia. It was the last straw for her when, one morning in early June, she opened the front door and it fell off its hinges. That was when Florence Magwaza decided that she would seek legal advice.

This was a move that was highly uncharacteristic of Florence. Florence had never before had any contact with lawyers or even considered that the solution to her problems might lie in legal recourse. It was a move born of desperation and motivated by advertising.

At about the same time that Florence's house began falling apart, a legal firm had started advertising prominently on television, especially on SABC1, which was the channel that Florence watched most often. The message that came across in their advertisements was that any misfortune could be blamed on someone else, and was potentially extremely lucrative. Thus, they instructed, if you had had any medical treatment that had not turned out as you expected, you would be foolish not to contact them to sue your doctor. If you had ever fallen in a shopping centre or slipped on a wet floor, you should contact the legal firm immediately to claim your compensation. They threw in an extra carrot: no win, no cost. Florence watched the advertisements and with each viewing became more and more certain that she could claim money from someone for repairs on her house. So convincing were the advertisements that the thought even entered Florence's head that she might be able to sue the company that had built her house for enough money to buy a new house. It was to this end that she called the toll-free number of the legal firm displayed on the advertisements.

It was a circumstantial chain of events that carried Florence's case from a dubious legal firm to the prestigious advocate Norman Ware. The details of how Advocate Norman Ware ended up representing Florence Magwaza in the cases of *Florence Magwaza* v. *Ubuntu Construction* and *Florence Magwaza* v. *the State* are superfluous to this story; suffice it to say that one of the attorneys who had been presented with the details of the case recognised that it involved high-profile political figures and allegations of bribery, corruption, irregular tenders and tax evasion, and had shunted the case upwards like a hot potato.

The details of the case landed on Advocate Norman Ware's desk in early July, at which time he had begun following up on the allegations. At the time of his murder, he had enough information to implicate both Titus Mokotla and VJ Maharaj. The first court appearance had been scheduled for the seventh of November. It was thus not wholly inappropriate that Detective De Villiers considered Titus Mokotla and VJ Maharaj to be high up on the list of suspects, especially since VJ Maharaj had at one stage owned the murder weapon.

Chapter Fourteen

Judith Dhlomo worked as a housekeeper for Norman and Elisma Ware. She had been employed by them for five years and during that time had stolen from them numerous pieces of jewellery, several items of clothing, twenty kilograms of washing powder and approximately R48,000. She had developed ingenious methods of getting her loot past the security guards who checked all the employees leaving the San La Mer estate: she hid jewellery and money in her underwear; she wore the stolen clothes beneath her own clothes; and she stashed the washing soap in her bra, after carefully decanting it into small ziplock bags. Because of the frequency with which she stole, Judith appeared to most who knew her on the estate to be at least two sizes larger than she actually was.

Judith had few qualms about stealing from her employers. Firstly, she needed the things that she stole from them far more than they did. Secondly, the Wares hardly appeared to notice when something went missing, which proved to her that they didn't really need the items in the first place. One didn't fail to miss essential items. And thirdly, the Wares personified for her both colonialism and apartheid, two systems that, although different, were merged into one evil in Judith's mind and on which she blamed all of South Africa's current ills, and, as such, she felt morally obligated to steal from the people who embodied for her the principles of these systems. Judith affirmed her actions by telling herself that she would never steal from the poor or needy, but as that opportunity had never arisen, it was difficult to determine the veracity of this avowal, and thus it was equally hard to judge whether Judith was intrinsically a bad person or not. Whatever the case was, Judith sold her behaviour to herself along the same principles as Robin Hood had almost nine hundred years before.

Because he was not involved in the day-to-day running of the household, and because he tended to be rather scatterbrained anyway, Norman Ware generally did not notice when something was missing, and when he did, he tended to blame it on himself rather than anyone else. Elisma Ware, however, had begun to suspect, by the fifth year of their employing Judith, that the housekeeper was stealing from them. Elisma had noticed that a few items of her jewellery had gone missing – pieces that she hardly ever wore but that were special nonetheless – and that more and more often she would arrive at the till at a shop to find less money in her wallet than she expected to. She also noticed that she went through washing powder at a far more reasonable rate over December, when Judith took leave, than during the rest of the year.

Elisma Ware found it inconceivable to confront Judith directly about the theft. The main reason for this was the very large burden of white guilt that Elisma carried around with her: she was as aware as Judith was of the inequalities of the past and the present. In fact, so heavy was this weight, this presence of history that Elisma carried on her shoulders, that it tainted every interaction she had with anyone who was black, effectively rendering it impossible for her to have a normal, uncomplicated relationship with anyone who had been previously disadvantaged. And so Elisma had to resort to sneaky and clandestine methods of catching Judith out. She started marking with a permanent ink pen the level of the powder on the bottle in which she kept her washing soap, in an attempt to measure how much was being used. She kept a diary of all the money she spent, so that she could keep track of how much was in her wallet. She even laid traps for Judith, 'accidentally' leaving pieces of jewellery lying around in the house or pretending to forget money in the pockets of her clothes. As complicated and time-consuming as it was, her spy work was pointless. There were two reasons for this. Firstly, Judith saw through the games: she avoided the traps and made her own markings on the bottle of washing powder beneath the markings that Elisma had made. Secondly, even if Elisma had found proof of Judith's guilt, she was unlikely to have had the courage to follow through on her findings.

Things might have continued in this state of suspicious and unhealthy inertia had Judith not stolen a pair of cufflinks that had been passed down to Advocate Norman Ware by his grandfather. They were simple gold chain-link cufflinks, and Judith had stolen them more because they had been easily available than because she had any desire to own an antique pair of cufflinks. She could not have sold them for much either, because their value was more sentimental than material. It was, however, entirely as a result of his emotional attachment to them that Advocate Norman Ware noticed they were missing. Initially he thought that he had misplaced them, but after Elisma turned out the safe and two of the drawers in her bedroom and checked the pockets of all of her husband's shirts and was unable to locate the missing cufflinks, Advocate Norman Ware became amenable to the idea that they had been stolen. The most likely, if not the only, suspect was Judith, and therefore this proved to be the ideal moment for Elisma to speak to Norman about her suspicions regarding their housekeeper. The discussion that they subsequently had took place in the bedroom, and the door was left open while they were talking. Judith could not figure out whether Elisma had simply forgotten to close it or whether she had purposely left the door open because she meant Judith to hear what she was telling her husband. Was it perhaps a kind of cowardly warning? Whatever the intention behind it, it worried Judith. She had not realised just how aware Elisma was of her stealing. She also had no idea whether Advocate Norman Ware would suffer from the same qualms of conscience to which Elisma was prey. Judith decided that it was best not to leave it to time or chance to find out. It was for this reason that after work that very day, she visited a witchdoctor in her hometown of Stanger, who went by the name of Mama Doctor.

For R250, Mama Doctor sold Judith a five-hundred millilitre bottle of muti that would ensure that her employers would be blind to her deception and thievery and that they would remain pliable to her manipulation. Judith was simply to add one tablespoon of the muti to their food once a day for it to take effect. This was easy enough, as Elisma had sent Judith on a cooking course to enable her to prepare the evening meals during the week.

Judith started adding the potion to her employers' food two weeks prior to the murder of Advocate Norman Ware. Of course, the concoction of powdered wild dagga, dried locust, nail clippings, Oros concentrate, and crushed Warfarin, Rifampicin, Fluanxol and Haloperidol was unlikely to have had any magical effects on the Wares. That both Norman and Elisma showed a sudden lack of concern for Judith's theft after she started adding the muti to their food had nothing to do with witchcraft and everything to do with the side effects of the medication that formed the backbone of Mama Doctor's brew.

Less than a week after Judith started contaminating their evening meals, Norman and Elisma Ware began feeling strange. Both of them started bruising easily and suffered from excessive daytime somnolence. Norman began experiencing debilitating dizzy spells, and Elisma had nausea and blinding headaches. Elisma made an urgent appointment with her naturopath to establish the cause of her symptoms and how to treat them, and was instructed to start a cleansing diet to rid her system of the mercury and parasites that were poisoning her. She dutifully bought a juicer and two kilograms each of beetroot, carrots, apples and spinach, and began a liquid diet of vegetable juice. Naturally, since she stopped eating the evening meals poisoned by her maid, she soon started feeling better. The bruising cleared and the fog of lethargy that had previously clouded her mind lifted. She tried to persuade her husband to join her on the juice diet; however, Advocate Norman Ware was of the opinion that naturopaths were quacks and continued to eat the food that Judith cooked for him. Ironically, had he listened to the naturopath, he might never have ended his life horribly mutilated on the floor of the men's bathroom.

It is testimony to the power of coincidence over science that the incidents of the two weeks prior to the murder of Advocate Norman Ware affirmed for Judith the dominance of the witchdoctor, and for Elisma the authenticity of the naturopath. Chance made of both of them avid and lifelong disciples.

———•———

In investigating the murder of Advocate Norman Ware, Detective De Villiers was faced with a unique situation. Because of the nature of the security estate on which the murder took place, he had a list of the people who had been on the San La Mer property on the night of the murder and thus had the names of all the possible suspects and witnesses. The connection of Titus Mokotla to the victim and, via VJ Maharaj, to the murder weapon narrowed down that list considerably, but Detective De Villiers still had to find proof to support his theory that Titus and VJ were involved in the murder. He was also fairly certain at this stage that they would not have been stupid enough to have committed the murder themselves, but would have paid someone else to do it for them, and so Detective De Villiers had the unenviable task of finding their lackey. He decided that it was time to start questioning the residents and staff who had been present on the estate on the night of the murder.

According to the list that he obtained from the estate security office, the house closest to the pool area, where Advocate Norman Ware was murdered, was inhabited by a woman with the name of Cordelia Cupido. Detective De Villiers reasonably assumed that if anyone had glimpsed the murderer or heard anything untoward around the time of the murder, it would have been Cordelia Cupido, in view of the proximity of her home to the murder scene. Of course, at the time he made that assumption he had no idea of the mental state of Cordelia Cupido.

When Detective De Villiers initially knocked on Cordelia's door and got no response, he went back to the security office to find out whether Mrs Cupido's disc showed her to be currently present on the estate. The security officer typed her name and address into his computer and told Detective De Villiers that Mrs C. Cupido was currently on the estate. As the officer scrolled down the screen, he commented that according to his records she had not left the estate for the past seven weeks. This flippantly mentioned fact immediately set Detective De Villiers's acutely honed mind on edge: it was not entirely normal behaviour for someone to remain at home for seven weeks, unless he or she was either under house arrest or dead. It was for this reason that when he went back to the house and knocked on the door again, and again got no response, Detective De Villiers opened the door and made his way into the house.

He was faced with the same disturbing and macabre scene with which Tariq Pillay had been confronted in his search for headache tablets. The house was dark and dusty and smelt like decomposition and decay. All the ventilation gratings, air-conditioning ducts, drains and windows had been sealed off with brown duct tape. Detective De Villiers felt the hairs on the back of his neck stand on end, and he phoned the estate security company to request that they send over a couple of security guards as backup.

When one deals frequently with certain circumstances, it is natural for them to become commonplace. So, where a layperson might automatically presume that a pregnancy should be healthy, a doctor might worry for the entire nine months about foetal abnormalities and maternal complications. Likewise, a homicide detective could be excused for thinking first about murder when faced with the situation in which Detective de Villiers found himself. It was thus initially a relief to Detective De Villiers when he opened the door to Delia's bedroom and found her alive.

One could argue that being alive is by no means an absolute. Technically it is – if one has a pulse and one is breathing spontaneously, one is alive – but subjectively it is a sliding scale ranging from 'barely alive' to 'full of life'. Delia was at the very bottom of the sliding scale. Detective De Villiers realised this as soon as he walked into the room. Delia showed the signs of being alive – her heart was beating and her chest moving – but her body was uninhabited. And Detective De Villiers could smell death in the air, beyond the stink of unwashed skin, rotting food and excrement. He pulled his cellphone from his pocket and dialled the number for an ambulance.

Delia had no comprehension of what was happening to her as paramedics stuck needles into her arms and pumped her body with life-saving fluids; as the same men loaded her onto a stretcher and drove her to hospital; as the casualty doctor peered into her pupils and ordered CT scans and X-rays and blood tests. She had given up on life and what happened to her body: the proddings and pokings and manoeuvrings meant nothing to her.

It took the physician a week to stabilise Delia enough to send her to the psychiatric ward. Although her physical condition had improved substantially, her mental state had not: she was alive, but remained lifeless. Her eyes roamed the room sightlessly. She was unable to speak. She didn't refuse food, but had to be fed as though she were a young child. No number of expensive and potent psychiatric drugs would be able to restore life to her because there was an elemental hurdle to her recovery: although her body persisted in performing its daily functions, her mind wanted only to be with her deceased husband.

It was while Delia was being pushed in a wheelchair from the medical ward to the psychiatric unit that she passed a young man on a gurney being wheeled to theatre by a neurosurgeon. The neurosurgeon was about to remove a large meningioma from the man's brain. It is unlikely that even if the patient had not been intubated and attached to numerous bleeping monitors, Delia would have recognised him as the security guard who had entered her house on the evening of the second of November.

———•—•———

There was a reason why Detective De Villiers was not investigating VJ Maharaj and Titus Mokotla, even though he was convinced that they were indirectly responsible for the murder of Advocate Norman Ware. Simply put, his stomach turned at the thought of becoming involved with two such highly politically connected people. He had no desire to be arrested, handcuffed in front of his family and dragged off to jail on fabricated or exaggerated charges.

Detective De Villiers was not generally considered a bad person. He had devoted most of his adult life to putting criminals behind bars, often at great risk to himself. Corruption among police officers riled him and he had never accepted a bribe, although he had been presented with numerous opportunities to do so. He was a conscientious father, watching both of his sons' rugby games on a Saturday morning, and a faithful and respectful husband. And if, on occasion, he had dealt a little too harshly with a suspect while trying to extricate sensitive information, or had perhaps been slightly trigger-happy while chasing a known murderer, he could hardly be blamed. He was, after all, working under highly stressful conditions – long hours, poorly trained staff above and below him, disgraceful pay, inadequate equipment – and dealing with the worst specimens of hardened killers, seasoned rapists and merciless hijackers. However, Detective De Villiers was under no illusion that these minor lapses of his would be ignored if he decided to investigate VJ and Titus further, and so his enthusiastic interrogating of every other potential witness in the case of the murder of Advocate Norman Ware was in truth nothing more than a very elaborate delaying tactic. Unfortunately for him, two events occurred while he was exploring other avenues that made it impossible for him to continue ignoring Titus and VJ and their connection to the murder of Advocate Norman Ware.

Chapter Fifteen

THE FIRST VISIT THAT Detective De Villiers made to Titus Mokotla's house was not to interrogate the great man himself, but to ask questions of his staff. He thus deliberately chose to conduct the interviews on a day that he knew Titus Mokotla to be away on business in Johannesburg.

The mansion in which Titus Mokotla lived was imposing. It was an ostentatious triple-storey building fronted by a large atrium lined with Corinthian-style pillars. Lights at the base of each of the pillars illuminated them at night. Titus had instructed his architect to give the house a casino-like feel and the columns were the result. Unfortunately, the resemblance was closer to that of a Roman temple than to a Las Vegas gambling house. This likeness to an ancient place of worship was not helped by the extensive use of marble on the exterior of the mansion.

The inside of the building proved equally disturbing to Detective De Villiers. As he entered Titus Mokotla's house, he felt as if he was walking onto the set of *GoodFellas* or *Carlito's Way* or *The Godfather* trilogy, or a combination of all three. Mafia memorabilia took prime position in the various display cabinets. Signed posters and photographs lined the walls. The only novels on the single bookcase were gangster tales. The man appeared to be completely obsessed with the American Mafia. For the first time, the thought entered Detective De Villiers's mind that perhaps Titus Mokotla had actually committed the murder himself. This was not the home of a stable man, and the mutilation that Advocate Norman Ware had suffered had undertones reminiscent of the torture meted out to the victims in Hollywood Mafia movies. Detective De Villiers, a man hardened by all sorts of vagaries of human nature, felt vaguely nauseous.

Titus Mokotla had a housekeeper and a gardener working for him on a full-time basis. It was from the housekeeper that Detective De Villiers learnt that the bronze cherub that had been used to murder Advocate Norman Ware had belonged to Titus Mokotla. The woman did not know who had given it to her employer, but she remembered that he had received it as a gift, along with many other artworks and some cases of wine, about a year before. She even volunteered to show Detective De Villiers where the statue usually stood, in the front garden beside a small fountain. She had not noticed that the statue was missing because she polished it only every couple of weeks.

Detective De Villiers's next question to her, about where her employer had been on the night of the second of November, seemed to throw the woman. She obviously realised only when the detective asked her about her employer's whereabouts on that date that he was implicated in the murder of Advocate Norman Ware. She hesitated a moment before answering, opening and closing her mouth a few times as though trying to catch the escaping words. Detective De Villiers reassured her that he would not dream of mentioning to Mr Mokotla that he had interviewed her. Of course this was untrue, but Detective De Villiers needed to know where Titus Mokotla had been on the night of the murder and whether he had an alibi. Eventually the maid spoke: she had not seen Titus on the evening of the second of November. He had not eaten the dinner that she had prepared for him and she presumed that he must have been out. But surely his wife must have eaten dinner, Detective De Villiers wondered aloud. The housekeeper fell into his neatly laid trap: there had been no one else at the house, she said; Mrs Mokotla and the children were in Johannesburg for the month.

Detective De Villiers left the interview feeling completely unsettled. The more information that he uncovered, the more likely it seemed that Titus Mokotla was involved in the murder. And now it appeared that he was dealing not only with a politically connected man, but with one who was also mentally unstable. For only the third time in twenty-six years in the police force, Detective De Villiers considered resigning.

The second event that persuaded Detective De Villiers that Titus Mokotla had, in fact, murdered Advocate Norman Ware occurred during his interview with Elisma Ware. Detective De Villiers interviewed Elisma Ware the day after he had questioned the Mokotlas' maid.

Elisma Ware opened the door for Detective De Villiers almost as soon as he knocked. Without appearing either theatrical or calculatedly histrionic, she was the perfect embodiment of the grieving widow. She was wearing make-up, but it failed to hide completely the redness of her eyes. She was dressed in a sombre grey skirt and black blouse that served only to highlight her pallor. Her manner was polite but subdued. She invited Detective De Villiers in and led him to the lounge, where they sat down on opposite leather couches. Elisma had met Detective De Villiers before, when he had questioned her initially, and she remembered that he liked black coffee with two sugars. She offered him a cup and, without waiting for his response, instructed the maid, who had been mopping the tiled floor, to make it.

Detective De Villiers had also been present when Elisma Ware had had to identify her husband's body at the mortuary. He recalled in detail how devastated she had been; how the colour had drained instantaneously from her face and she had gripped the edge of the metal gurney to prevent herself from falling over when the assistant forensic pathologist lifted the cloth covering Advocate Norman Ware's head, revealing his disfigured face. Detective De Villiers had indicated to the assistant not to lift the cloth any further than necessary because of the effect that her husband's mutilation would be likely to have on Elisma. She did not need to see what the murderer had done to his hands, feet and genitals. It was because she had already suffered so much shock that Detective De Villiers spoke to Elisma with more compassion and empathy than was usual for him, and he was particularly careful not to disclose in their subsequent conversation any details that might upset her further.

Since Elisma Ware was not a suspect in the case, Detective De Villiers did not feel the need to record his conversation with her, but if he had, the transcript would have read as follows:

E.W.: So, are you any closer to finding ... to closing the case?

Det. D.V.: I believe we are. We're very close to finding the perpetrator now. I was wondering if you had any additional information for us that might help. Anything that your husband was working on, perhaps? Any specific people who might not have wanted him around?

[*It was not Detective De Villiers's intention here to ask a leading question. He simply wanted to make efficient use of his time.*]

E.W.: You know, it's so difficult. His line of work ... well, there are always people who don't want him around. He got death threats before, you know. But come to think of it, there might be something. I've only just remembered it now that you ask. My husband received a brown envelope a couple of days before ... before it all happened. The letter inside seemed to upset him a lot. It must have been something important because he kept it locked in the drawer in his study where he keeps sensitive work documents. He started acting strangely after he received that envelope. There's no doubt in my mind that it upset him. You know, I'm so silly: I didn't actually think about it until now. I can get it for you, if you like. It might be nothing, but maybe it's worth looking at.

Det. D.V.: Please. Anything will help.

The brown A5 envelope with which Elisma Ware returned contained a vital piece of the evidence with which Detective De Villiers would prove Titus Mokotla's guilt. The evidence was a letter, written by Titus Mokotla to Advocate Norman Ware, dated the twenty-third of October 2011. It had been written by hand

and the handwriting would be confirmed, in court by a forensic handwriting expert, to be that of Titus Mokotla. Detective De Villiers could not help wondering at the lack of foresight that his suspect had shown in writing a threatening letter by hand, and signing it. But then, the letter on the whole was completely bizarre, dotted with malapropisms and inappropriately placed proverbs, and could hardly have been the work of a rational or stable person. Were it not for the tragic undertones carried by the murder investigation, the letter might have been comic: a hyperbolic rendition of the typical threatening letter in a B-grade gangster movie.

[Exhibit H: the letter]

23 October 2011

To: Advocate Norman Ware

I have warned you before this to leave the case of Florence Magwaza alone. This is the last time that I will warn you. If you do not listen to this warning you will face <u>die consequences!!</u> I repeat: <u>I will not warn you again!!!</u>

I know why you do what you are doing. It is because you are <u>jealous</u> of my power and my money. You do not like to see that a <u>black</u> man is succeeding more than you a white man. You want wealth and power only for whites like yourself. I warn you that I am amorous with many powerful and inconsequential people. I have friends in high places that can <u>take you down</u> and squash you like the dirty little fly that you are!! Remember: <u>Blood is thicker than water.</u>

You accuse me of stealing money. Let me tell you that you and your descendants have stolen the land and the money of my people for the past 400 years. We are only taking back what is <u>righteously ours</u>. Do you dare to defy me that right? Believe me, I will take this further. I will not let it rest. Remember: <u>The rolling stone gathers no moss!!</u>

What you are saying about me amounts to nothing more than <u>label charges</u>. Beware about what you say: defacement of character is no small charge. I will fight fire with fire. I will deface you. I warn you that I am a strong and powerful man. I am like the <u>black Godfather</u> and my people are everywhere. You cannot hide from me. I will <u>destroy</u> you!!! By the time I am finished with you, you will be emasculated. You will never be able to look at anyone again. You will not have a foot to stand on. I will tear you apart <u>piece by piece</u>. Remember: <u>Revenge is sweet!</u>

Know that <u>God is on the side of the righteous</u>. If you do not hide my warning, He will surely send his emissary down to strike you dead. <u>DO not ignore me</u>: you will <u>sorely</u> regress it.

Regards

Titus Mokotla

The knuckles of the hand in which Detective De Villiers was holding the letter turned white as he read; he was sure that Advocate Norman Ware would have taken the obscure threats figuratively. There was no way that Advocate Norman Ware, an apparently sane and reasonable man, could have known that the author of the letter had meant the threats literally.

In television shows there are special crime-scene investigation units that scour a crime scene for clues and evidence. In real life, there are seldom such luxuries, and so the scene of the murder of Advocate Norman Ware was examined by Detective De Villiers and two of his juniors, as well as a state assistant forensic pathologist. It was a relatively new investigator, Detective Choudry, who had taken swabs of the blood that was found at the scene of the murder. In the case of the murder of Advocate Norman Ware, it would have been ridiculous for all the blood to be sampled, since the large amount of blood pooled around the victim obviously belonged to the victim. Detective Choudry had taken a routine random sample simply to confirm this. Of far greater interest was the fact that there had been a few drops of blood on the floor near the basin, peripheral to where the body lay, and Detective Choudry had focused on these splatters. The hope was that they were splatters of blood from the perpetrator, who might well have injured himself while killing and mutilating Advocate Norman Ware. It was Detective Choudry who phoned Detective De Villiers, an hour and twenty minutes after he had finished his interview with Elisma Ware, to tell him that the DNA from the peripheral blood splatters on the bathroom floor did not match the DNA of the victim.

There are two commonly used methods of analysing DNA from blood found at a crime scene: polymerase chain reaction (PCR) and restriction fragment length polymorphism (RFLP). The forensic scientist analysing the blood specimen sent in by Detective Pillay used the latter. If the DNA of a blood sample taken from a suspect were to match the DNA extricated from the crime-scene specimen, it would place the suspect at the crime scene. RFLP DNA is statistically individualising to one in several billion and has withstood rigorous court challenges to its validity. Thus, if Detective De Villiers wanted to close the case against Titus Mokotla, he would need to obtain a blood sample from him. The legality of obtaining a blood specimen from a suspect is tricky and complicated, and Detective De Villiers knew that it would be even more so than usual in the case of Titus Mokotla. He removed the cellphone from his pocket and dialled the number of the office of the state prosecutor assigned to the case.

———•———

Even before she found the body of Dumazile, Noluthando had resolved that this would be the last sale of body parts that she would make. The process of cutting up dead bodies had become too traumatic for her, especially after this last incident.

Occasionally, when the lady for whom she cleaned had a dinner party, Noluthando stayed over for the night in the servant's quarters, so that she could serve at the dinner table, clean up after the party and babysit the children the following morning while her employer nursed a hangover. She had waited and cleaned up at such a dinner party on the evening of the second of November. It had been an unusually raucous party, fuelled by an expensive white powder, and the guests had left only at around three in the morning. Noluthando had finished washing dishes and wiping up vomit at approximately four o'clock. Because she had felt too agitated to go to sleep, she had decided to take a walk to calm her mind. Ironically, her walk would do anything but that.

Noluthando had ambled up from the cul-de-sac in which she worked, onto the main road, Kingfisher Drive. The dawn was perfect: still and balmy, with the sun just starting to light up the horizon, and Noluthando had continued walking, following Kingfisher Drive until she reached a parking lot. Usually she would have turned around there because, as a staff member, she was not actually allowed to wander about the estate, but the security guard had been asleep on the bench and so she had made her way to what appeared to be a pool area.

Noluthando never regretted her decision to go for a walk, or even her choice to continue past the sleeping guard into the perfectly manicured pool area, but she bitterly regretted going into the men's restroom to use the toilet. She should have walked the fifty metres further and gone to the ladies' toilet (she had, after all, already walked just under two kilometres), or squatted in the bushes, or even held her bladder tight until she got home, but instead she had decided to pop into the men's toilet quickly before turning back, which was how she stumbled upon the body of Advocate Norman Ware.

Initially, Noluthando had thought that the man lying on the bathroom floor had passed out drunk – bear in mind that this would not have been the first man that Noluthando had seen passed out on a bathroom floor that evening, and so the scenario had become quite commonplace for her. It was the pool of blood around the man's head that hinted at something more suspicious than simple intoxication. Noluthando approached the body cautiously to check whether the man was breathing or not.

On finding that the stranger was dead, Noluthando's first instinct had been to wake the security guard, but in the three minutes that it took her to get to him she had changed her mind. Not only would waking the security guard raise all sorts of unwelcome questions about what she had been doing in the men's bathroom in an area of the estate that she was prohibited from being in, but the thought had entered her mind that she might make a profit from the situation. Noluthando slipped past the somnolent security guard and hurried back to her room to fetch some gloves, her pruning shears and a plastic shopping bag in which to put the harvested body parts.

Previously, Noluthando had removed digits and appendages from bodies that had been preserved in formalin. The job had elicited some revulsion in her, but it had been relatively clean, and because of the greyish colour and the unusual texture of the formalin-embalmed flesh, she had managed to pretend to herself that she was working with plasticine. This was not the case in her harvesting of the body of Advocate Norman Ware. Not only was the corpse of Norman Ware relatively fresh, but he had been fed exceedingly high doses of Warfarin prior to his murder, and so blood that would usually have been clotted was still very fluid. By the time that Noluthando had finished chopping off Advocate Norman Ware's fingers, toes, penis, scrotum and facial extremities, she was covered in blood. The whole process disgusted and revolted her. Besides that, it took longer than she had expected, and so she was worried the entire time that the security guard would wake up and catch her in the act of mutilating a corpse. Fortunately for Noluthando, the benzodiazepines made sure that Tariq slept through her activities and she was able to smuggle the body parts past him before he awoke.

Noluthando ran back to her quarters, an eerie, bloodied

spectre trying to hide from the light, and immediately got into the shower fully clothed. She used a scrubbing brush and a bar of Sunlight soap to scrub the blood off her body and her clothing. As she watched the pink water swirl down the drain, she swore that this would be the last time that she would touch a dead body. The only thing that had got her through the horrific deed was the consolatory thought of how much money she would make from the escapade. There was high value placed on male genitals.

It was for this reason that she was so bitterly disappointed when she got to Mama Doctor's door later that morning and no one responded to her knocking. Noluthando stared at the bag of mushy, plastic-wrapped body parts she was carrying. What was she supposed to do with them? She knew instinctively that they would not keep as the other ones had, but would soon start to rot. She would not be able to keep stinking body appendages hidden. She knocked on the door more forcefully, but still there was no answer. The thought occurred to Noluthando that she could leave the bloodied body parts in Mama Doctor's room and ask for her money later. She tried pulling down the door handle, and to her surprise the door swung open. It was as she entered Mama Doctor's rooms that she saw the witchdoctor's body on the floor. Noluthando started whimpering and shaking at the sight of her second dead body in less than forty-eight hours. She dropped Advocate Norman Ware's extremities on the floor and ran from the room, closing the door behind her.

Noluthando was too afraid to go home immediately. She understood that she had been cursed for her actions, for her harvesting of body parts. She worried that if she went home, she might find one of her family members lying dead on the floor. She convinced herself that she had inadvertently killed both the stranger in the bathroom and Mama Doctor. Her greed had made her into an angel of death. She wept as she sat in the taxi, oblivious to the concerned looks and sympathetic hands of her fellow passengers.

Eventually, like so many before her, Noluthando would find her consolation in religion. In a dramatic display of remorse and self-flagellation, she would make her confession and ask for forgiveness. Noluthando would live the rest of her life walking on the straight and narrow path of the righteous. It would never occur to her that she should perhaps have donated the money she made from selling body parts to the church, or that she should have told the police about the buried bodies, and about her mutilation of Advocate Norman Ware's corpse. Her guilt was not powerful enough for her to endanger her freedom, her job or her comfort over it. Had she done that, had Noluthando contacted law enforcement officers and made her confession to them instead of a lay preacher, she would have influenced history in two important ways. First, the police would have been a step closer to finding one of South Africa's most notorious and elusive serial killers, and second, the case against Titus Mokotla would not have been quite as strong.

Contrary to what Noluthando believed, Dumazile Dlamini's death had had nothing whatsoever to do with her. Dumazile had died as a result of a prolonged epileptic seizure. She had gone downstairs, as usual, when she had smelt oranges, but outside the building there had been a bakkie offloading some citrus fruit to the wholesaler, and so Dumazile had made her way upstairs again, attributing the smell to the delivery. In a strange coincidence, the oranges had arrived simultaneously with Dumazile's aura, obscuring her premonition of a seizure. She had started convulsing soon after returning to her room. Had the oranges arrived a few minutes earlier or later, she would have been in public when her seizure occurred and there would have been witnesses to phone an ambulance, dramatically increasing her chances of survival.

Chapter Sixteen

PEOPLE IN HIGH PLACES with whom Titus Mokotla had previously been friends would have been able to protect him had the charges against him been charges of corruption, libel, bribery or simple assault. They would probably even have been able to get him off charges of rape, judging from past successes; however, they were unable to get him off a charge of murder. Quite frankly, even they were rather disgusted when the full details of the case were exposed. The general consensus was that obviously the man had lost his mind and it was far better for him to be locked away safely in prison than to be out and about where he might further sully the name of any of his friends.

Titus Mokotla continued to claim his innocence, even though the evidence against him was overwhelming. He had had a motive to kill Advocate Norman Ware, which he had stated in a letter to the victim a few days prior to the murder; he was the owner of the bronze cherub that was used as the murder weapon (the fact that the torture instruments were never located was generally ignored); and splatters of his blood had been found at the scene of the murder, attesting to his having been present there; and yet he continued to insist that he had been asleep in his bed on the night of the second of November. Titus Mokotla's lawyer tried to persuade him to undergo a psychiatric evaluation in an attempt to prove that he was not of a sane state of mind when he committed the murder, but Titus refused. And so the arguments that Titus's lawyer presented to the court were embarrassingly weak: he had written the letter as an empty threat and he had meant nothing serious by it; he was the owner of the statuette, but the last time that he had seen it, it had been standing innocently beside a fountain in his front garden; and the blood on the floor of the men's bathroom was from a cut on his finger that he had sustained on the afternoon of the second of November. There were no witnesses to his injury. In fact, the only witnesses to his actions on the second of November – the manager of the restaurant at the pool area and two of his waiters – claimed that when they left the pool area at around six p.m., Titus had been alone there in an inebriated state.

Although the case against Titus Mokotla was watertight, and Detective De Villiers was happy that he had caught the perpetrator and that there was enough convincing evidence to ensure he would be convicted, there was one small thing that still bothered the investigator. He could not forget the momentary guilt that VJ Maharaj had displayed when the topic of the bronze statuette had been brought up at his initial interview. Also, VJ Maharaj was one of Titus Mokotla's most avid and vocal critics once Titus was arrested, and yet he kept very quiet about the fact that he had given the murder weapon to Titus Mokotla a year prior to the murder (a fact about which he had lied). This did not escape Detective De Villiers's notice. He did not know whether VJ Maharaj was connected to the killing of Advocate Norman Ware or whether there was something else that he was hiding, but he knew that it would be dangerous to begin questioning him too enthusiastically. The same people who had denounced Titus Mokotla would not be so quick to betray VJ Maharaj. There were a couple of reasons for this other than the fact that VJ had not obviously committed a bizarre murder, not least of which was the fact that VJ still made large donations to the political party to which he was affiliated.

Detective De Villiers mulled over the problem for a few days. He made some cursory enquiries into VJ Maharaj's interests, but none of them yielded any information of significance. Eventually he decided that he should be satisfied with having caught the murderer and that he would leave VJ Maharaj to implicate himself in another crime.

Approximately ten months after Titus Mokotla was sentenced to life imprisonment for the murder of Advocate Norman Ware, VJ Maharaj found himself the subject of an extensive audit by the receiver of revenue. Little came of it, apart from the fact that VJ Maharaj developed hypertension, for which he would remain on lifelong treatment, and that he was forced to pay a very large fine for tax evasion, which ate into his liquid assets considerably.

Whether the South African Revenue Service decided to audit VJ Maharaj because he had failed to declare an income for the past ten years, or because they had received a tip-off from the betrayed and embittered Titus Mokotla, or because one of Detective De Villiers's cousins worked as an accountant for the revenue service, is impossible to determine.

Contrary to what the residents of the San La Mer estate feared, the lead story in all the daily newspapers on the third of November was not about the murder of Advocate Norman Ware. The anxious residents could rest assured that their property prices and business interests remained, for the moment, unaffected. The lead story on the third of November was a sensational exposé about the plastic surgeon Dr Phillip Landers. The fact that he was actually a San La Mer resident was unimportant because his defamation did not in any way adversely affect the reputation of the estate.

Since he had never received Narges McIntyre's voice message, Dr Phil was oblivious to the imminent publication of the article detailing his sexual proclivities, his unethical practice and his overcharging. He went to work as usual on the third of November and saw his first three patients. It was only at about ten o'clock, when his receptionist brought him a cup of coffee and a copy of the *Daily News*, as she always did, that he became aware of the article. Had Dr Phil been less egotistical and self-absorbed, he would have noticed the smirk on his receptionist's face as she placed the paper in front of him, and would not so readily have attributed her hanging around in his office to her wanting to be near him. It was a surreal moment for Phillip Landers when he opened the newspaper and was faced with a large colour photograph of himself. His immediate thought was that it was some sort of practical joke, except that it was not April Fool's Day. It was only when he read the headline, 'Pervert Plastic Surgeon Scams and Shags Patients', that he realised the implications of the article. It was also then that he noticed for the first time the smugness of his receptionist's expression. He barked at her to get out of the room, which she did, fairly skipping, and Phil stared at the page, trying to make sense of the words swimming in front of his eyes.

It was far worse than Dr Phil could have imagined; worse than the incident in Cape Town. With a sinking heart he realised what a field day the media and the Health Professions Council would make of this. There was no depth that the author of the article – a Vincent Schreiber (Phillip Landers vaguely recognised the name but couldn't place it) – had thought too private to plunder. There was mention of the twins he had screwed on his operating table one evening; of the woman for whom he had created a double vagina, both of which, once healed, he had personally tested; of his unorthodox use of gynaecological instruments; and of his penchant for Barbie-doll lookalikes. Then, of course, there was the more serious issue of the fraudulent billing.

Phillip Landers was a broken man. He sat at his desk, his head in his hands, and wondered how life could be so bitterly unfair to him. It was beyond his level of insight to realise that he was responsible for all that had happened to him; instead he blamed his downfall on the journalist who had written the article, the newspaper that had published it, the Health Professions Council, Viagra, the media and life in general.

Fourteen months after the publication of Vincent Schreiber's article and the fulfilment of Narges's revenge, a plastic surgery practice opened in a dodgy private hospital in Zimbabwe. It was run by an Eduard Domingo, MD, who claimed to have studied in the Ukraine. No one bothered to check up properly on his credentials. The clinic was called Re!nvent Yourself.

Justice has a strange way of asserting itself. There is little doubt that Titus Mokotla deserved to go to jail. He was corrupt to the core; had on numerous occasions accepted bribes and kickbacks, not least the R1.2 million that VJ Maharaj had paid him in artworks, wine and cash as part of the subsidised housing scam; could easily have been accused of racketeering; and had already had several charges of sexual harassment laid against him. However, he might well never have seen the inside of a jail cell had it not been for the unlikely set of circumstances that led to his being convicted of the murder of Advocate Norman Ware.

There were a great many people, Detective De Villiers not least among them, who felt immense satisfaction in Titus's conviction: it was proof that action begets consequence and that right still has the upper hand. Their comfort was an illusion, for although Titus did indeed deserve to go to jail, he did not deserve life imprisonment. He was telling the truth when he claimed to be innocent of the murder of Advocate Norman Ware.

Was it this desire for order that had biased Detective De Villiers's judgement or was it the detective's preconceived convictions that had misdirected him? Had his acumen been clouded by the pressure he was under from his superiors to close the case as quickly as possible? One can never be one hundred per cent sure. Perhaps it was just that his armour had cracked slightly to reveal the universal human tendency to make mistakes. Whatever it was, Detective De Villiers had missed a very important clue in his investigation into the murder of Advocate Norman Ware. The clue was the whereabouts of the key to the drawer that had contained the brown envelope. Detective De Villiers had presumed that Advocate Norman Ware had kept the key to his study drawer where it was accessible to Elisma. He hadn't bothered to ask the apparently innocent grieving widow how she had unlocked the drawer that had contained the letter from Titus Mokotla.

Chapter Seventeen

So what was the sequence of events that led Elisma, the most unlikely, the most unusual of suspects, to murder her husband? Perhaps it makes the most sense to start with the brown envelope.

On the twenty-seventh of October, Elisma Ware received a slip from the post office stating that there was a registered letter waiting for collection. The letter was addressed to Advocate Norman Ware, but it was usual practice for Elisma to collect registered letters for her husband, signing for them with her identity book. Elisma Ware collected the letter on the twenty-eighth of October and handed it, unopened, to her husband that evening. It must be emphasised that there was nothing out of the ordinary about this situation; Elisma often collected letters for her husband, who frequently received registered letters. It was also perfectly usual for Advocate Norman Ware to open the letter and read it in front of his wife, often discussing pertinent issues with her, as they sat in the lounge having their glass of wine before dinner. What was unusual was the reaction that the letter elicited from Norman Ware. He stared at the letter for a few moments with a look of bewilderment, confusion almost, on his face, and then hastily put it back into the envelope.

Without saying a word to Elisma, he went upstairs to his study. Elisma hovered behind her husband, getting to the study just as her husband locked the letter in his private drawer and replaced the chain and key around his neck.

Elisma felt strangely betrayed. She wondered why, if the contents of the letter were so important to her husband, he had not shared them with her. She liked to believe that there was no information, either personal or professional, that her husband withheld from her. (Over the many years that they had worked together, Elisma had become her husband's sounding board. There was little that he did not discuss with her, and she liked to believe that he conferred with her because he valued her input; that her opinion was worth as much as, or more than, that of his colleagues.) She did not ask Norman Ware about the letter, but she felt its presence between them, like an uninvited guest, for the rest of the evening. Elisma was not to know, at that stage, that the look of bewilderment that her husband had displayed on opening the envelope had more to do with the author of the letter's use of malapropisms than with the letter's content, and that her husband had not bothered to discuss the letter with her because he thought it ridiculous and did not want his wife to worry needlessly over the absurd threats. She was also not to know that Advocate Norman Ware's strange behaviour the following week, which she associated with and attributed to the arrival of the letter, was actually the result of the psychoactive substances that her maid was feeding her husband, and was not related to the contents of the letter in any way.

Be that as it may, Elisma could not forget about the letter. The more she tried to remove it from her mind, the more it worried her, until she was completely obsessed with finding out what the envelope contained. It might well have been that the obsession had more to do with the fact that her husband was, for the first time to her knowledge, hiding something from her than with the letter itself, but the brown envelope came to symbolise for Elisma the worst betrayal of trust.

Elisma tried hinting about the letter to her husband, in the hope that he would divulge the nature of its contents, but he appeared immune to her persuasions. She asked him repeatedly what the matter was, but he avoided talking about the letter and attributed any aberration in his behaviour to his feeling unwell. Twice, at night while her husband was sleeping, she tried to remove the key from around his neck, but Norman Ware was a light sleeper and both times he woke before she was able to accomplish anything. Of course, Norman Ware's refusal to divulge the contents of the letter was an attempt to protect Elisma from unnecessary worry, but she was not to know this. Elisma began building up a fanciful and completely unfounded notion that her husband was having an affair and that the contents of the envelope were being used to blackmail him. That was the only plausible reason Elisma could find to explain her husband's reluctance to discuss the letter with her.

Why did Elisma choose this specific betrayal of trust to become obsessed with? Is an affair the generic, almost default, form of betrayal in a relationship? Or was it a specific fear that Elisma had, perhaps born of the fact that she had had a philandering father? There is also the possibility that Elisma might have feared a carnal betrayal because of the sexlessness of her and Norman's marriage. Was she carrying around a subconscious guilt?

Whatever it was, over the following week Elisma

became more and more suspicious of every one of Norman's moves. She checked all of his telephone messages and read the emails on his computer. She phoned him at odd times, demanding to know where he was and what he was doing. His innocence only served to confirm for her that he was a master of deception.

By the morning of the thirty-first of October, Elisma had worked herself up into such a state of emotional turmoil that she booked a double appointment with her psychologist. The consultation between Elisma and her psychologist ranged from an abstract discussion of the nature of true love to whether Elisma would be able to, or would want to, divorce Norman Ware should she find out he was having an affair. After two hours of talking, Elisma returned home with her thoughts far better organised. She had resolved that she would not mention the affair to Norman. The nature of true love, she had decided, was that such love should be unconditional. Her love for her husband, then, should remain unchanged regardless of his behaviour. This was a noble but completely untenable notion. Not once did Elisma question the basis for her assumptions regarding her husband, or entertain the possibility that her husband might be innocent of any form of betrayal.

During the day of the second of November, Elisma's fears were confirmed in a dramatic and indubitable way. True to her resolve, she approached the proof of her husband's betrayal with an apparent elegant calm on the whole. Her concerns, at the end of the day, were more for her husband than herself.

On the morning of the second of November, Advocate Norman Ware woke up feeling disoriented. He felt as though he lacked proper depth perception, so that everything looked either further away or closer to him than it actually was. He also felt inexplicably agitated. Had he been asked, he would have described the anxiety as being similar to that which one experiences prior to an important exam. Was this a premonition of what was to happen later? It may have been, but it was far more likely to have been a side effect of the medication he was unwittingly being fed.

Advocate Norman Ware phoned his chambers and told them he would be off for the day and then called his general practitioner, with whom he made an appointment for the following day. Breakfast and a cup of coffee failed to settle Norman. It was a useless exercise for him to try to work on his computer in the condition in which he found himself, so he put his papers aside and made his way upstairs to his bedroom. He put on an old pastel-blue tracksuit and some running shoes and went outside in the hope that some fresh air might help. As he walked out of the door, Elisma warned her husband that it looked as though it might rain, but he appeared not to hear her. He left the house at half past ten.

By eleven o'clock, a light drizzle had started falling and Elisma decided to go and fetch her husband in the car. The motive behind her action was not to check up on his whereabouts, but to bring him home before he got too wet. She did not want him getting more ill than he already was. She took his car, a silver Mercedes, and drove down Kingfisher Drive in the direction of the pools, as this was the route her husband usually walked. Elisma Ware passed Norman at the parking lot beside the pool area. He did not notice her because he was walking towards the pools with his arm around a woman. Elisma, who had spent so many years studying the man who was now her husband, was able to read in a glance the intimations of Norman's body language: they showed concern, protectiveness and, most of all, absorption. She continued driving until she thought the couple were out of sight, and then did a U-turn and drove back home.

The drizzle had turned to rain by the time Elisma got home, and as she stomped into the kitchen, she passed Judith bringing the clothes in from the washing line. The weather echoed Elisma's mood. Within minutes lightning pierced the heavy clouds, releasing torrents of water from them. Elisma imagined it was blood. Thunder grumbled and snapped in agony.

Elisma had never considered herself to be racist, but she could not help balking at the thought of her husband with a black woman. She realised, at that moment, that for all her talk of equality, for all her apparent liberalism and her outspoken support of multiracial relationships, she was, at heart, no better than the architects of apartheid had been. Unwelcome images popped into her head, taboo images the origin of which she was unaware: pictures of peppercorn pubic hair; of flushed pink penis penetrating purple-blue labia. The images disgusted her. They engendered in her an almost physical revulsion. Elisma walked out of the kitchen door into the storm. She stood with her arms outstretched and her face turned up to the clouds, willing the rain to wash all feeling from her. Her husband passed her on his way back into the house, he as wet as she was, and mentioned that he was going to lie down for a while. Elisma did not acknowledge having heard him, nor did she ask him where he had been. She concentrated on the pricks of the rain falling on her face. Had Advocate Norman Ware been of a clearer frame of mind, he would have questioned Elisma's standing in the rain, but in his befuddled state he failed to appreciate the abnormality of the situation.

Summer storms pass quickly. Within as little as two hours after a storm has raged, all evidence of it can have disappeared. It is as though it has never happened and all of nature has returned to its pre-storm equilibrium. By one o'clock, Elisma had overcome her fury and disgust. She had re-uttered the avowals of unconditional love that she had made earlier in the week. She brewed herself a cup of chamomile tea, dissolved half a bottle's worth of Rescue Remedy tablets under her tongue and resolved to meet calmly whatever else the day brought her. This was just as well, because she was to face three more disturbing situations before the sun set that evening.

The first happened soon after she had finished her cup of chamomile tea. The telephone rang, but because Elisma had just downed half a bottle of Rescue Remedy tablets she was slightly slow in reaching the landline. The telephone had switched to voicemail before Elisma could pick up the receiver, and Norman had not answered because he was asleep in bed. Elisma waited for a couple of minutes and then dialled the telephone mailbox. There was one new message.

Elisma listened to the message and suspected immediately that it must have been left by the same person who had sent the brown envelope to her husband. She had never heard such anger, such cold fury, in someone's voice. The woman, who only ever referred to Norman Ware as 'you pig', was threatening his professional ruin; gloating that she had divulged all the sordid details of his harassment of her to the newspapers, and that the article would be the lead story the following day. This was a progression that Elisma Ware had not anticipated. She had, rather vainly she now thought, believed that the lever for the blackmail would have been her, the unsuspecting wife. But this was far more sinister. This woman, this hate-filled banshee, was putting Advocate Norman Ware's career and reputation at risk. If she had been asked, Elisma Ware would have denied worrying that the article would put her reputation at stake as much as her husband's; she would have shrugged off any intimations that this was information that she would prefer her friends and acquaintances not to know. Elisma would have been emphatic in her assurance that her concern was all for her husband, but is one ever totally immune to the opinion of others? Is it possible to place a value on one's good name, and once sullied, can it ever be fully restored?

An individual's emotional make-up is unassailably complex. Emotions twirl around in one's psyche: they sit one upon the other, one intertwined with another, one hiding or one exposing another, until they are impossible to separate, to define in their essence. Thus it is a difficult task to ascertain which emotion it was that drove Elisma's actions for the next twenty-four hours, if indeed it was a single emotion. Was it anger at her husband for his betrayal of her? Or was she acting altruistically, driven by righteous indignation? Was it protectiveness for her husband that motivated her? Love? Hate? Is there much of a difference?

———

Elisma might not have noticed the lingerie were it not

for the brilliant turquoise-lilac colour of the lace. She had subconsciously migrated to the basket of washing brought in by Judith earlier in the day and had started folding it in an attempt to take her mind off her husband's affair. Some of the washing was wet and needed tumble-drying, but other items of clothing were dry enough to be folded or ironed, and Elisma was distractedly sorting through them when she glimpsed the electric hue of the corset and knickers. She knew immediately that the lingerie must belong to her husband's mistress. She presumed that Judith had mistakenly thrown the underwear in with the general washing, reasonably assuming it to belong to her employer. Elisma fingered the delicate lace and smooth satin ribbon thoughtfully. She tried to imagine the woman who had worn the underwear for her husband. Was it the lady she had seen him with earlier or was there someone else? She wondered what it would feel like to have Norman strip the knickers and corset from her body; whether she would feel self-conscious and dirty or whether, against all odds, she might enjoy it. And where had they done the deed? Had it been in her bed? The guest room? The sitting room?

Strangely, finding the underwear did not trigger in Elisma the same fury that seeing Norman with another woman had done earlier in the day. Whether this was because she had resigned herself to the fact of his affair, or because she had used up all of her anger, or because of the overdose of Rescue Remedy that she had taken, is impossible to tell. Elisma folded the underwear neatly and placed it in a plastic bag that she then stashed in a cupboard in the laundry. She had no idea what she was planning to do with the lingerie; whether she intended one day to try it on or if she was keeping it for a time that she would need evidence against her husband. All that

Elisma was sure of was that it did not feel right to throw the underwear away.

***

Advocate Norman Ware slept for most of the day. He woke up in the late afternoon expecting to feel better, but the agitation that he had felt earlier in the day had not completely resolved. He had had strange dreams while he slept: vivid, hallucinatory chimeras full of characters from long-forgotten childhood stories. The dreams left him feeling even more disoriented than he already was. Previously he had been confused as to place; now time seemed out of joint as well. He felt as though he was intermittently slipping back into his youth. He stumbled downstairs and made himself a cup of coffee. Although the caffeine did little to help the agitation, it did wake him up and displace the disorientation. By the time he found his wife, folding washing in the laundry room, he was feeling almost normal again. He certainly felt better than he had the whole day. He asked her if she wanted to join him on his usual late-afternoon walk, but she declined the offer, so he set off on his own.

When he returned from his walk forty minutes later, Norman Ware was unaware that the perfume worn by the little lost girl he had carried home had rubbed off on him. Elisma smelt it on his clothes as soon as he came near her. Naturally, because the perfume belonged to the girl's mother and was an adult fragrance, Elisma Ware presumed it had been transferred onto Norman's skin from the neck of one of his mistresses. She couldn't help wondering at his callousness at having asked her to join him on his walk.

———•———

It was strange that over their six years of marriage, Elisma should find no evidence of her husband's infidelity and then, in one day, she should see him with his arm around another woman, get a suspicious telephone call from a slighted mistress, find a lover's underwear in her home and smell the unfamiliar scent of a strange lady on him. One has to question whether she was looking too hard. Had the thought that her husband was having an affair lodged itself so deeply into her conscious mind that she was unable to be objective in her appraisal of the evidence?

It would not have been unreasonable for Elisma, based on what she believed to be damning evidence, to have packed a bag and booked into a hotel room for a couple of nights, or to have thrown plates at her unfaithful husband, or even simply screamed and shouted at him. It was, if not unreasonable, then odd that she simply sat down to dinner with him, as she did every evening at seven o'clock, without mentioning the events of the day. She sipped her beetroot-and-carrot juice while Norman ate the chicken stew that Judith had prepared for him.

———•———

Probably because he had slept for most of the day, Norman Ware struggled with insomnia on the night of the second of November. He tossed and turned in his bed, pulled the duvet over him and then, five minutes later, kicked it off. Elisma attributed his restlessness to a guilty conscience, but she too, with a clear conscience, was unable to sleep. Unbidden images of her husband with other women appeared as soon as she closed her eyes. Some of the women were black, others white; he was taking some on the desk of his office and others in an unfamiliar hotel room. The turquoise-lilac lingerie glowed against the black of her eyelids.

When her eyes were open, she worried about what the following day would bring. She wondered what secrets would be let loose in the article, whether there would be photographs of her husband's mistress or mistresses, and how she, the betrayed wife, would be perceived. She worried that her husband would be debarred, prohibited from practising law any more. Elisma considered telling Norman about the phone call but decided against it. Her reasoning was sound: there was nothing that he could do ' about it in the middle of the night and it would just cause him unnecessary worry. Besides, if she started talking about all that had happened, she didn't know whether she would be able to keep to her vow of unconditional love; whether she would be able to contain the monster of fury that boiled beneath her calm exterior.

When, in the early hours of the morning, Norman got up and made his way downstairs, Elisma found it impossible not to follow him. She waited, feigning sleep, until he had gone out of the front door, and then followed silently.

In going outside at three o'clock in the morning, Norman Ware had no ulterior motives. The dose of medication that Judith had fed him with his dinner had begun to take effect and his agitation had returned. He wondered whether he was developing flu because he seemed unable to control his body temperature. In fact, it was purely because he was so hot that he went outside. He had not meant to walk, but once he was outside the cool air felt pleasant and the movement of his legs soothed the agitation. And so he made his way, with no hidden agenda or cryptic design, to the pool area. Elisma walked stealthily behind him, his nocturnal shadow.

———

One of the police force public relations officers had described the bronze cherub used to kill Advocate Norman Ware as a weapon of chance or opportunity. It was not the type of weapon chosen as a result of extensive planning, unless there was specific significance attached to it. Rather, it was more likely to have been easily at hand.

Elisma noticed the bronze statuette as she walked past the garden of Titus Mokotla. If asked, she would not have been able to say why she went and picked it up. It might have been because, as she walked past it, the rays of the moon illuminated the smooth curves of the plump metal limbs, as though placing the cherub in a spotlight for her to see. It might equally have been because it was easily accessible. She would have claimed, had anyone asked her, that she had had no plan at that stage. It was only while she was following her husband to what she thought was a clandestine lovers' meeting, she would have stated, that she decided on a course of action.

———

Murder is entirely in the intention. It is intention that differentiates murder from manslaughter. Why is it so important that there is this differentiation? What is the weight of intention? The end result, after all, is the same: a life prematurely lost. The reason is that the *intent* to kill implies a deficiency in conscience. To be able to conceive of purposely taking another human being's life, except in a situation of self-defence, suggests a psychopathic trait. Plainly put, there is necessarily evil in murder.

Elisma Ware would never be convicted for the murder or the manslaughter of Advocate Norman Ware, so it is a moot point to try to ascertain whether she intended to kill her husband or simply to disable him. Was the blow on the head that she gave him – a light blow, fatal only because of the toxic levels of Warfarin in Advocate Norman Ware's bloodstream (of which she was unaware) – intended to make it appear as though Advocate Norman Ware had fallen and hit his head? Indeed, had his body not been mutilated, foul play might never have been suspected. Advocate Norman Ware had been complaining to colleagues of feeling off balance, and had made a doctor's appointment to ascertain the cause of his vertigo, so it would not have been completely implausible for him to have fallen and knocked himself unconscious. This would have landed him in hospital, where he could conveniently have ridden out the public and professional outcry that Elisma anticipated would follow the publication of what she believed to be a damning article.

There is evidence to support both sides of the argument. On one hand, Elisma had no idea that the security guard would be asleep, which would suggest that her intent was not murder, and her choice of the statuette was hardly a prime example of a well-thought-out murder weapon. She was also, as mentioned previously, unaware that her husband was the victim of Warfarin poisoning. On the other hand, Elisma was emotionally fragile. The man she had loved and revered, to whom she had essentially devoted her entire adult life, who she knew had never once cheated on his first wife, and whose affection she had worked so hard to gain, had betrayed her in the most vile and disrespectful manner, and it would have been completely understandable for her to have hit her husband a little too hard, or one too many times on the head. She knew, after all, that there were witnesses to his recent vertigo, and that a fatal fall would be entirely believable.

It is impossible to determine whether Elisma killed her husband intentionally or whether, ironically, his death was a by-product of her trying to protect him from the fate she believed lay in wait for him the following day. And it would probably be irrelevant, except for the fact that manslaughter is far less likely to be repeated.

Chapter Eighteen

Advocate Norman Ware's funeral was well attended. Not only were many of his colleagues present to pay their respects to a well-regarded member of the profession, but so too were many of the clients that Advocate Norman Ware had helped over the years. The latter formed an eclectic assortment of people, many of whom had had to search old pockets or the bottoms of handbags for forgotten change in order to pay for transport to the San La Mer estate, which was where the memorial service was being held. They too wished to mourn the passing of a good man and perhaps to thank him one last time. Of course, many of the San La Mer residents were also at the funeral, although they were drawn to it more because of the macabre and sensational nature of Advocate Norman Ware's death, and the associated melodrama that comes with it, than out of any respect for the deceased.

Elisma Ware was wearing a simple black trouser suit and black court shoes. Her head was bare. It irritated her that some of the attendees at her husband's funeral, people she knew had attended only because of the media presence, had thought the occasion an opportunity to make a fashion statement. One such person was the platinum-blonde woman wearing a black cocktail dress and a swooping black, feathered hat who approached Elisma as soon as the service was over. Elisma vaguely recognised her from the pages of the San La Mer social magazine as Cherise Andreakos. Elisma tried to escape, but she was hemmed in by people on all sides. It was only as Cherise came nearer that Elisma saw the young girl in tow. She looked about five or six years old.

It was as the blonde stranger leant forward to give Elisma a token hug that Elisma smelt the scent. There was no mistaking it: it was a sweet scent, slightly cloying, with undertones of cinnamon and orange; the scent of the perfume that Elisma had smelt so distinctly on her husband. Instinctively, she withdrew from the woman's embrace. She wondered at the blonde's audacity, to come and hug the grieving widow of the man with whom she had been having an affair. It was so callous that it was almost unbelievable.

Elisma's eyes darted to the girl. She was looking down at the ground, obviously bored by her mother's histrionic search for attention. There was something fragile about her; a neediness that was impossible to ignore.

The woman was blowing her nose and opened her bag to offer Elisma a tissue. It was almost as though she thought that since she and Elisma had shared the same man, they were now friends. Sisters-in-arms, so to speak. Elisma excused herself: it was too much to bear. She wanted to get away from the woman and the scent.

Elisma did not think about the young girl again until later that evening. She was looking at the photograph of her husband on the front of the printed funeral handout. It was blurred and grainy – the photocopy had not picked up the detail of the original photograph – and slightly squashed, leaving Norman Ware with a plumper, rounder face than he had had. It was while she was staring at this warped photograph that she noticed the resemblance between her husband and the young girl.

In truth, there was little resemblance, apart from the fact that both had brown eyes. Any similarities between the two faces were in Elisma's imagination only, and because of that, the more that Elisma stared at the photograph, the more she saw a likeness to the young girl at the funeral. By the following morning, she had managed to convince herself that Emily was the result of a liaison between Norman and Cherise Andreakos.

This theory of Elisma's was entirely fictitious. There was not a single piece of evidence to support it, and a great deal of evidence to support the fact that Emily was Mr Andreakos's child. So why did Elisma latch onto it? The answer, perhaps, lies in her response to her imaginary scenario.

Elisma showed no anger at all towards Cherise Andreakos. In fact, she was indifferent to her existence. All of her attention was focused on Emily. She took it upon herself to ensure that the girl she believed to be her dead husband's daughter was being raised properly. It is likely, then, that in making Emily Norman's child, Elisma was finding a replacement for her husband; someone on whom to shower her now unattached affection and love. Unwittingly, she chose the perfect candidate. Emily felt so abandoned that she would cling to whatever love and attention she could find.

Elisma started working on her relationship with Emily slowly. She would walk past Emily's house, and if the young girl was playing outside, she would stop and have a conversation with her. Sometimes she might point out interesting things to Emily, such as a weaver's nest dangling from a branch, or a dried snakeskin that she had picked up the day before, or a miniature brightly coloured sunbird piercing an aloe bloom with its curved beak. Once Emily was more comfortable with her, she would invite Emily to her house, where they would do activities together: colouring-in or baking or sorting stickers. She taught Emily to knit, and Emily knitted herself a rather rudimentary pink scarf. On occasion, Emily would bring her homework with her on her visits to Elisma, and Elisma would help her work through the problems. Soon it became routine for Emily to walk up to Elisma's house every afternoon.

Elisma never spoilt Emily. On the contrary, she was relatively strict with her young mentee. When Emily visited Elisma, there were routines that had to be adhered to, such as Emily always washing her hands before eating, and taking her plate to the kitchen once she was finished, and tidying up after an activity. These rituals and routines, which are so taken for granted and yet so despised by most children, gave Emily a sense of order and security that her home atmosphere lacked. And so it was only natural that as she grew older, she came to spend more and more time with Elisma.

Eighteen years later, when Emily Andreakos would graduate from the University of KwaZulu-Natal with a degree in law, *summa cum laude,* she would invite only one person to her graduation ceremony: Elisma Ware. By then, Emily had long been accustomed to calling her 'Mother'. Was there anything unnatural in this? Elisma Ware had, after all, given Emily the childhood that she might otherwise never have had. She had been far more of a maternal figure to Emily than Cherise Andreakos was, and so why should she not have had the privilege of being called mother? It is very unlikely that Emily would have finished school or graduated from university had it not been for Elisma's influence. Elisma Ware had never treated Emily as anything other than a daughter, and it would take a bitter and cynical person to point out that Elisma's obsession with Emily was a little too reminiscent of the infatuation she had had for Advocate Norman Ware.